The Angel Factory

The Angel Factory

Terence Blacker

SIMON & SCHUSTER BOOKS FOR YOUNG READERS
NEW YORK LONDON TORONTO SYDNEY SINGAPORE

SIMON & SCHUSTER BOOKS FOR YOUNG READERS
An imprint of Simon & Schuster Children's Publishing Division
1230 Avenue of the Americas, New York, New York 10020

First published in Great Britain by Macmillan Children's Books
First U.S. edition 2002

SIMON & SCHUSTER BOOKS FOR YOUNG READERS is a trademark of Simon & Schuster.
Book design by O'Lanso Gabbidon
The text for this book is set in Garamond.
Printed in the United States of America
2 4 6 8 10 9 7 5 3 1
Library of Congress Cataloging-in-Publication Data
Blacker, Terence.
The angel factory / by Terence Blacker.—1st U.S. ed.
p. cm.
Originally published: Great Britain: Macmillan Children's Books, © 2001.
Summary: Spurred on by his best friend, twelve-year-old Thomas uncovers two major family secrets: that he was adopted, and that his perfect-seeming family is part of an other-worldly organization.

ISBN 0-689-85171-5

[1. Adoption—Fiction. 2. Family life—London (England)—Fiction. 3. Angels—Fiction. 4. Extraterrestrial beings—Fiction. 5. London (England)—Fiction.] I. Title.
PZ7.B53225 An 2002
[Fic]—dc21   2002001262

To Caroline Sheldon

1 · FAMILY

I CAN SEE US NOW, that morning, the sun shining through the kitchen window, lighting up our little family group at the breakfast table.

My father was reading a geography project on supermarkets that I had been working on for the last month. He had helped with some of the early research and the previous night I had printed out my final version on his computer.

A radio was playing, with some discussion over a big political meeting that was taking place in London the following month. Dad stirred slightly and, with that weird thought-reading process that my parents have, my mother stood up and switched it off.

Almost immediately, as if to fill the silence, there was a growling sound from under the table. Dougal, my white West Highland terrier, had found his toy woolen rabbit and was killing it once more.

"Oh, Dougal." My mum laughed, reached down to pick up the rabbit and put it on a sideboard. "What d'you think?" she asked my father as she washed her hands in the sink.

Dad sighed and closed my project, shaking his head as if it were the worst thing he had ever had to read. Then, joke over, he looked up at me and smiled. "Excellent," he said. "Absolutely excellent." He stood up and placed the folder in front of me, laying a hand on my shoulder. "I'm very proud of my son."

"Cheers, Dad," I said, my mouth full of cornflakes.

My mother glanced at her watch. "We're going to be a bit late tonight," she said. "Amy is gracing us with her presence for dinner."

"Oh, great," I muttered.

"No need to be rude about your big sister," said Dad automatically as he cleared the plates from the table.

It was time for them to go to work. They kissed me, each of them. Mum reminded me to lock up carefully and not to be late for school. I saw them to the front door. Shouting goodbyes, they made their way up the garden path, Dougal bouncing at their feet, in the morning sun.

I walked back to the kitchen and picked up my project. My father was right. It was excellent.

Everything was excellent.

2 · GIP

WE WERE ON THE SWINGS that afternoon, Gip Sanchez and me.

There was nothing particularly unusual about that. Gip was my best friend. On the way back from school, we would often go to the park and chat about things. Only, on this occasion, we did something different.

We talked about my family. Now and then an adult would walk by, glancing at us as if to say we were too old to be in this part of the playground, that we must be up to something.

That's the way it is when Gip's around. He gets glances. Before he says a word, there's a sense of anger about him, with his long, shaggy hair, his dodgy skin, his dark eyes, his odd way of walking.

Life has never been kind to Gip. He was born with one leg shorter than the other. Before he was a year old, his dad left home. The way he tells it, his mum is more interested in God, alcohol, and herself (not necessarily in that order) than in her only son. He gets beatings in the playground like other people get school dinners.

There's something about Gip, a sort of pleasure in his own weirdness, that seems to annoy people within seconds of meeting him. It's not just that he shuffles about like a creature from another world but that he goes out of his way not to fit in. He actually likes to look disgusting. When some of the older kids at the school took to calling him "Gimpy" because he limps, and then "Gyppo" because there is something of the wild gypsy to him, he took the name "Gip" as if it were a special prize that had been awarded to him.

Which made them even more annoyed.

Which made Gip even more determined to be Gip.

In the end, people at school have learned to treat him with a sort of edgy respect. In spite of everything life has thrown at him, Gip's a winner. He knew about computers before anyone else. He was the first in school to have a mobile phone. Sometimes, when he talks about things, he seems ten years older than he is—in experience, in life.

No one quite understands why we are friends—Gip Sanchez, the well-known geek and neighborhood oddball, and Thomas Wisdom, a bright, normal kid from a bright, normal family. My parents, so easy about everything else, are not easy about this. Ever since they met Gip at a parents' evening, they wince when I mention his name.

Maybe that was why I liked him, why our friendship was so strong—it owed nothing to anyone but ourselves.

Maybe it was why, that afternoon in the park, I talked to him about my family.

"Sometimes I envy you," I said.

Gip swung backwards and forwards in silence, head down, his hair concealing his face.

"You can just be you," I said. "You've got no one to disappoint—no one to live up to."

"Yup," said Gip. "I've got to admit that it's all pretty great."

"I'm serious. You don't have to belong to this perfect family. You don't feel that, however well you do, it will never be quite as good as your parents expected."

Gip looked up, surprised. He had never been the biggest fan of my family but he knew it was unusual for me to talk about them like this.

"If I do anything well, I feel I've kind of borrowed my success from my family," I said. "And if I don't, the failure's all mine."

"That's families for you," said Gip. "I've never seen the point of them, myself."

"Sometimes I wish they would get drunk now and then." I laughed guiltily. "Or lose their tempers. Or shout at me when I do something wrong. Everything's so perfect in their lives. They even hold hands in public."

"Weird," said Gip.

"Everything has to be done together, as a family, this great Wisdom family team. They work together. We go to California for our holidays every year together. And you know what I've noticed recently? That they even go to the lavatory every morning at the same time. One after another. Everything they do is so orderly and . . . regular."

Gip was looking at me oddly.

"I don't make a habit of studying these things," I muttered. "I just notice stuff."

"Maybe it's not you that's out of step, but them," he said in the worryingly quiet voice which usually means that he has begun working on some strange, Gip-like theory. "What did you say they do for a job?"

"Food development. They don't tell me much about it."

"Of course they don't," said Gip thoughtfully. "They wouldn't, would they?"

"Why not?"

Gip jumped off the swing. "CIA," he said, almost to himself. "I've been reading how spies operate. Often they're the most ordinary people. In fact, the more ordinary they are, the more likely it is that they're some kind of spook." He turned and began walking towards the gate.

"Spook?" I was following Gip now, regretting that I had told him anything about my family.

"Are they at your place now?"

"They're working late."

"Perfect." He accelerated, with that odd swinging stride of his. "Let's go."

3 · SPOOKY

AS WE MADE OUR WAY to the house, I tried to explain to Gip that I wasn't exactly being serious. I had been in a bad mood all day because, although I knew my geography project would get an A, I felt the mark was not mine but my dad's. I said that it had all been a joke but, in Gip's upside-down world, anything serious is really a joke in disguise while what most people would see as a joke, he takes with deadly seriousness.

I realized that I had made a big mistake confiding in him about my parents. Then I made an even bigger one. I let Gip into my house.

As soon as we entered the hall, he asked to see my dad's computer. Still trying to play along with his little game, I showed him upstairs.

Moments later, he stood in the center of my father's small, super-tidy office, looking absurdly out of place, like some giant bit of litter that had been blown in from the street.

"My parents are kind of into neatness," I explained.

He took in the scene, the rows of folders on shelves, the filing-cabinet, the immaculately tidy desk. "It's plain unnatural," he muttered, sitting down in front of the computer. "It's spooky."

"Not everyone has to live like you," I said, suddenly resenting the way Gip mocked anyone whose life was not like his.

He switched on the computer. "Code-word," he said quietly. "We need a code-word to get in."

He tapped in my name, waited a few seconds then muttered, "Nope."

"Dougal?"

"Eh?"

"It's the name of my terrier."

Gip shook his head as he typed in the letters. "Your life, man," he muttered.

Nothing.

As if I weren't there, Gip opened the top drawer of my father's desk and took out an address book. He opened it at the first page. "What's the Seraph Organization?" he asked.

"Something to do with my parents' work. They're the food company that employs them."

Gip's fingers flew over the keys.

Nothing.

He returned to the address book, studying one page after another.

I glanced at my watch. "Gip, they'll be back soon. I'll be so dead if they find you here."

He ignored me. "Who are SO?" he asked suddenly.

"Search me."

"More to the point. Why does their telephone number have only five digits?" He tapped the numbers into the computer. Suddenly the screen came alive.

"Welcome," said a friendly cybernetic voice.

"Welcome to you," said Gip.

We were in.

Gip is one of those people who never feels more at home than when he's in front of a computer. Within seconds, he had called up my father's files. They read:

HOME

BILLS

SERAPH

TAX

"Gip, this is wrong," I said. "There's nothing here."

He opened "SERAPH."

It was full of letters from my dad about schedules, visits, advertising, deadlines—as dull and innocent as any business file could be.

Before I could stop him, he opened "HOME." It was stuff about insurance and rates.

"So much for the CIA theory," I said.

But Gip had double-clicked on "TAX." The screen suddenly filled with numbers—five pages of batched numbers, like a telephone directory without the names.

"Good thinking, guy," he muttered. "Nothing could look more boring and innocent than the old tax file. But you didn't fool old Gip." He closed the file. "OK," he said. "We print these out and then we leave."

"It's just some kind of tax thing," I said and I realized how absurd it all sounded. The truth was that, if my dad really did have some kind of secret life, I was suddenly not sure that I wanted to know about it.

"Knowledge is power," said Gip, pushing the "Print" key. "Now," he said, as the printer whined into life. "Where's this lavatory of yours?"

I told him and waited by the printer until it had finished spewing out pages full of numbers. When I had switched off the computer, I made my way downstairs to my room.

There are times when I forget just how weird my friend Gip is. After about five minutes, it occurred to me that he was spending more time than was entirely usual in my lavatory. I knocked on the door and asked if he was all right.

He said something but his voice sounded odd and echoey so that I couldn't catch the words. Then I noticed the door was not fully shut. I pushed it and nervously peered in.

Gip was on his knees in front of the lavatory. He looked like a headless man.

"What you doing, Gip?" I didn't know whether to leave him or to help.

His voice echoed weirdly from the depths of the lavatory bowl. "Uuggghh."

"Are you feeling sick?"

"I'm uunngghh," he said impatiently. Slowly, he emerged from the bowl. He stood up and shook his head. At the same time, both of us noticed that the ends of his hair were wet. Gip squeezed a few strands and wiped the palms of his hands down the sides of his jeans.

"Spies use lavatories to conceal information. I thought maybe there was some kind of secret hiding-place. That was why your parents are always slipping off to the bog—they're filing a report." He lifted the lid off the cistern.

"I was joking," I said desperately. "They were just going to the toilet like anyone else. Let's—"

"Yes." It was a low groan of triumph. Slowly he extricated his hand. He was holding a small, flat, black rubber plug.

"Well done, Gip," I said. "You just mashed up our plumbing."

"At the back of the cistern, there's a small metal plate."

He put his hand, still wet, on my shoulder and, with the other, pointed downwards into the water. There was, it was true, an oddly colored plaque behind the ball cock.

"It's called a bolt, Gip," I said. "It's what plumbers use."

"Yeah, right. And they use copper and cover it up with rubber. I don't think so." He opened the window that was just above the lavatory and, standing on the bowl, peered downwards.

When he came back into the room, he was smiling. "Transmitter," he said. "The bolt has a connection outside."

He returned the plug to where he had found it and put the lid back. This time he dried his hands by running them through his hair.

"You were right," he said. "Your parents are CIA. They're communicating to headquarters using the old lavatory trick. I was right. There's definitely something spooky going on here."

I sighed. At that moment, it seemed pointless to remind him that I had never ever claimed that my mum or dad were in the CIA, that all I had said, casually, was that I felt a bit out of place in my perfect family. It had been a joke and it had backfired and I wanted Gip to leave my house before he got any other crazy ideas about my family.

"They'll be back soon," I said. "You'd better go."

He picked up the sheaf of papers we had printed from my father's computer and waved them significantly in front of my face. "With the evidence, right?"

"Yeah, of course. With the evidence."

He glanced at me and winked—I may not be good at hiding my thoughts but luckily neither is Gip too good at reading them.

He limped his way to the front door. "It's good you brought ole Gippy in on this," he said. "We'll crack it together, right?"

"Sure," I said, eager to get shot of him. I glanced up and down the road. The coast was still clear but, at any moment now, my mum and dad would be rounding the corner from the station.

"All you got to do is check the precise times when your folks go to the john," he was saying. "Then, casual-like, try to listen outside the door, catch any noises in there that are kind of unusual, and leave the rest to me," he said.

"Right. I'll remember to do that."

I watched as he walked off with that swift scuttle, his right leg jerking outwards as if he were kicking out at some invisible thing with every stride. Then, suddenly I saw them. Walking towards him were Mum, Dad and, between them, my sister Amy with Dougal scuttling along ahead of them.

Briefly, I had this creepy sense that I was looking at two types of human—walking away from me, the frail, the strange, the sick and, walking towards me, the strong, the healthy, the normal.

My family turned into the short path leading to our front door. Dougal jumped up to greet me.

"Hi, Thomas," said my father. "What are you doing here?"

"I thought somebody rang the bell. Then I saw you."

My mum kissed me. "Amy's here to discuss the holiday," she said.

My sister kissed me too. "Hi, bruv," she said.

"Hi," I said.

I was glad that they were home. I glanced up the road to see Gip turning the bend, and began to relax.

We went inside for tea.

4 · NATURAL

ONCE, WHEN MUM, DAD, AMY, and I were returning from a walk in the park with Dougal, a neighbor, old Mr. Godwin from three doors down, was in his front garden. He looked up as we approached.

"What a lovely family you are," he said.

"Thank you, Mr. Godwin." My mother smiled politely but kept walking.

"You look like a band of angels," he called after us.

My father laughed, adding quietly, "If only he knew."

It was true, thinking about it later, that my mum and my dad look pretty good, considering their age. Most of my friends' fathers, for example, are a bit crumpled and battered—they've lost their hair, their waistline is history, whatever. But my dad, without making any particular fuss about it, looks like he's in shape. He's tall and has an open, smiling face, which people seem to trust. Not that he's vain about his appearance—he gets his light, sandy hair cut about once a month, goes to the same clothes shops, works out now and then at the gym. He's just one of those people whose looks don't change much as they get older.

If I told you that my mum has long blonde hair that comes down to the middle of her back, you might get the wrong idea. She's not some aging bimbo, or an old hippy who believes in astrology and feng shui and listens to Bob Dylan every night. She just likes her hair long. It suits her, makes her look natural. When she visits school on parents' day, I notice the way the male teachers (even nutty old Rendle, our math master) react to her. Normally they sit, slouched and grumpy, at their desks. As soon as Mum walks in, they straighten their backs, try (almost always unsuccessfully) to look like real men of the world. Yet, as soon as she starts talking in that quiet, reassuring voice of hers, they relax. She has the knack of making people feel better about themselves, more interesting and attractive than they really are.

Luckily, my sister Amy has not been back to school since she left three years ago. If she had, there might have been a riot. These days, even I have to admit that she looks good. Three years of success at university has given her a sort of glow of confidence. No way is she any kind of show-off but, when she enters a room, heads turn. "My daughter, the blonde bombshell," Dad calls her.

And me? Sometimes I wish I were like Gip and was able to go around, a walking mess of shabbiness, without caring, but the fact is, when Mum buys me nice clothes, I wear them. If I haven't had my hair cut for a few weeks, I begin to feel uncomfortable. I'm not a Nigel Neato—my room's as trashy as any of my friends' rooms (with the exception of Gip's which is literally a rubbish dump)—but, if you saw me out walking with my family, you would see the connection, all right, and I'm not ashamed of it. And yes, my hair is kind of blond too.

So Mr. Godwin, our wizened old neighbor, took one look at us and saw angels.

At the time, I thought his brain was out to lunch. These days, I'm not so sure.

5 · OXYMORON

A BLACKBIRD WAS HIGH in the poplar tree over-looking our garden, singing above the mur-muring sounds of the city, as the four of us sat at the garden table. There was some-thing in the air that evening. My father had opened a bottle of champagne. Amy was home. It was just like old times.

Dad raised a glass. "To Amy and her bril-liant degree," he said.

My sister smiled. "Maybe we should wait until we get the result," she said, but no one was fooled. Somehow, with Amy, the result has never exactly been a problem.

My mother held her glass in the air. "And to Thomas and his supermarket proj-ect. Another triumph," she said.

"Er, not," I mumbled.

They allowed me another half-glass of champagne. We chatted easily about school. Mum brought out pasta and Dad made one of his famous salads, over which we all cooed and clucked as if no one had ever made a salad before. The blackbird sang on as the sun went down. It was almost as if some trick of fate had created the perfect reply to Gip's crazy theories about my family.

We were well into the evening when my sister sprang a surprise on us.

"This holiday," she said, "would anyone object if I brought along a friend?"

We must have looked a little startled because Amy blushed. "All right," she said. "So I didn't tell you I've been seeing someone."

"Hold the front page," I muttered.

"Thomas." My mother gave me the look of mild warning—head tilted, eyebrows raised—that I knew so well.

"But it's not exactly big news," I said. "Jack. Rufus. Alex. The big news would be if she wasn't seeing someone."

"Ignore him, Amy," said my father. "Thomas will understand these things when he gets to university."

"Anyway, it's different this time," Amy said quietly.

Mum laid a hand on Amy's. "Tell us all about him," she said.

"He's a surfer—"

The three of us groaned in unison, then laughed.

"An intelligent surfer," said my sister.

"Intelligent surfer?" said Dad. "That sounds like an oxymoron to me."

"He's not a moron," said Amy. "He's very bright and good-looking and nice and I want him to come to Santa Barbara with us."

I was expecting objections from my parents. We have always done things together, as a family—not just the holiday in California but events at school or university. When one of us is playing in some team, or acting in a play, the other three will come along, show support. The rest of the world is beyond our little unit. As if only the best is suitable company for any member of the Wisdom family, Mum and Dad have always been wary and worried about who we pick as friends.

"He'll pay for himself," said Amy. "He's been saving up."

"He's just into that West Coast surf," I said.

"He says he's not going for the surfing." There was a new, wobbly smile on my sister's face. "He wants to be with me."

"Oh, puke," I said, just loud enough to be heard.

"Well, I think it's an excellent idea," said my mother decisively. "If he's brave enough to put up with us, I think we should take him."

"He can tackle twenty-foot waves, so I don't think the Wisdom family will be a problem," said my sister.

"You won't just hang out with him all the time, will you?" asked my father. "You'll be around for evening meals."

"Yes," said Amy. "But he's not exactly a conversationalist. He's sort of . . . quiet."

"The strong, silent type," said my father. "I like the sound of this man. What's his name?"

"Luke. Luke Ross."

"Tell us more," said Mum.

So we were treated to a little, damp-eyed version of the life and times of Luke the surfer-boy. How he had dropped out of university and traveled the world in search of the perfect wave. How any girl who had ever met him fell in love with him. How he worked in a hire-shop in Torquay when he wasn't riding surf. How, one day last summer, Amy had been down in the West Country with a couple of friends and had walked into Luke's shop and how it had first been a friendship thing, then became a bit more than a friendship thing, and now they met up every weekend.

It didn't take a genius to tell that my sister was more serious about this guy than she had been about any of her other boyfriends. When she had finished talking, we sat in silence for a moment, each of us thinking about how our little holiday group of four had just become five.

My father smiled at me. "Thomas, are you OK about Luke coming along?" he asked. "This is your holiday as well."

"No problem," I said. "He sounds . . . just great."

Every night, for as long as I can remember, my mother would sit on the edge of my bed before I went to sleep. She would read from a book, or tell me about things from her childhood in the country or just chat about little, everyday events. The words she said mattered less than the sound of her voice, soft and soothing and reassuring as sleep crept up on me.

There was a distraction that night. I heard my father going up to his office. He stayed there five, maybe ten minutes.

When he came downstairs, he looked into my room. Over my mother's shoulder, I saw him standing there at the door, looking at me, and in that moment I sensed not only that Dad knew about my visit to his office with Gip and that he knew that I knew, but that something—something I was unable to understand—was about to change forever.

Mum turned to see him and some kind of unspoken message seemed to pass between them because she squeezed my hand, kissed my forehead and turned out the bedside light.

I lay on my side and closed my eyes. Then, for some reason, I opened them again after a few seconds. My parents were standing together at the door, two shadows silhouetted by the light outside.

"What?" I raised my head. "What is it?"

"Night, old boy," said my father, and they left me there in the darkness.

6 · SPYBUSTER

THE END OF THE SUMMER term was approaching. I was looking forward to my holiday, even if the idea of Surfer-Boy tagging along with the family had cast a small, wave-shaped cloud over my thoughts. Both Dad and Mum seemed to be paying particular attention to me and, for a while, I wondered whether, having found out about about my inviting Gip back home, they were trying to guilt some kind of confession out of me.

Then I relaxed. Sometimes when my parents become more caring than usual, it can get on my nerves—their attention hangs on me like a weight—but now they seemed at ease, as if, without knowing it, I had passed some kind of test and was halfway to being treated like an adult.

I was OK. They were OK. Everything was going to be fine. I began to think that my worries about their being unusually ordered and perfect was my problem, not theirs. Maybe I had got depressed during the long summer term, or something at school had bothered me.

All would have been fine were it not for one Gip Sanchez, private detective and spybuster.

Some people take one look at Gip and take him to be some kind of loser. I know better. He likes to act chilled and laid-back but in reality he's as relaxed as a limpet. When he catches hold of something—an idea, a person—he hangs on until he is ready to let go.

I was that person. The idea was that my mother and father were fully paid-up members of the Central Intelligence Agency and were beaming messages back to America through our toilet. There was nothing I could say to shake this obsession from his head.

"It's an encryption thing," he called out to me as I made my way through the school gates one afternoon.

"What?" I may have allowed my irritation to show in my voice.

"Encryption." Gip loped along beside me, ignoring my pathetic attempt at disapproval. "It's a sort of code used in computers, logarithmic formulae to represent letters in the binary code or standard numerical form."

"Gimme a break, Gip. I'm not in the mood for a math lesson."

"Exactly," said Gip, who was clearly so excited that he was no longer receiving any messages from the outside world. "So all we need to do is, like, de-encrypt the encryption code and we'll find out what's in your father's secret file."

"Maybe we should forget it," I said. "It could be something just private and embarrassing."

Gip frowned as if this possibility had not occurred to him. "Yeah, what happens if it's some kind of creepy membership of the freemasons or something?"

I laughed. The idea of my dad belonging to a secret society was pretty wild, even by Gip's standards. "You don't know my father," I said coldly.

We walked on in silence for a few seconds. "So in the end," said Gip in a casual tone of voice that made me immediately suspicious. "I talked about it to Rendle."

I stopped in my tracks. I had always known that Mr. Rendle, the greasy-haired geek with stained trousers who taught math at school and whose nickname was "The Beast," was one of Gip's few other friends but not for a moment had I considered that he might actually share our silly little secret with him. "You did what?"

Gip shrugged. "Only the theory," he said. "I was chatting to him about encryption during break—"

"You are a sad person," I muttered.

"—and I brought the subject around to the way you break down codes. There are various degrees of difficulty. To put it simply, an encryptive logarithm working within conventional algebraic parameters can be resolved by—"

"Gip." I had stopped walking again. "Just put my mind at rest here. Have you or have you not shared a private personal document stolen from my father's computer with The Beast?"

Gip winced. "Only in so far as I lent it to him," he said.

"You what?"

"He promised to let me have it back. He doesn't even know where the pages came from. It's not a problem."

I had stopped walking. There was no point in being angry with Gip, or trying to explain why handing Dad's file over to a dorky math teacher felt like a betrayal. It was a family thing and Gip didn't do families. "Get it back." I spoke quietly.

"All right." Gip held up both hands in surrender. "I'll

get your precious numbers back."

"I want you to destroy everything we got from my father's computer."

"What about the CIA?"

"Gip."

He shrugged. "Suit yourself."

I walked away.

"Coming to the park?" he called after me.

I kept on walking.

Three days later, on the very evening after school had broken up for the summer, my big sister decided to introduce her darling surfer to the family.

They came to dinner—Amy smiling and blushing and casting adoring, proud glances in the direction of her boyfriend and Luke, tall, sandy-haired, blue-eyed, and mostly silent.

It was not an easy meal. My mind was too full of Gip's big mistake for me to want to talk much. Luke was one of those annoying, confident guys who seem to think that reasonable looks, floppy hair, a suntan and broad shoulders are enough to get him through life. He could leave it to lesser mortals to do the conversation thing.

He answered my mother's polite questions with answers so short that they were a hair's breadth from being openly rude.

Yeah, he was really into traveling.

Working in his shop was all right except when he had to deal with gonks who didn't understand the sea.

Sure, he surfed in winter. Like, a wetsuit? He'd caught some of his best waves in, like, January.

Nope, he hadn't thought about a long-term career. Like, carpe diem ("That's 'Seize the day,'" my sister added helpfully).

And, yeah, he was totally into the idea of coming to California. He had always wanted to hang out with the stars on Sunset Boulevard, you know?

Amy greeted this last remark as if it was the greatest witticism she had ever heard. My mother and father laughed dutifully but, for some reason, I forgot to join in.

Surfer-Boy fixed me with his piercing blue eyes as if, in his great worldly wisdom, he understood how I felt. I held his look for a few seconds. He winked in that patronizing way of adults, then gave a craggy smile to my sister who was simpering away beside him.

Great. Suddenly, we had a total airhead in the family.

7 · CALIFORNIA

IT WAS A GOOD HOLIDAY. It was a fine holiday.
It was always a fine holiday when we were in
Santa Barbara. We swam and watched dol-
phins and toured a studio in Hollywood.
We paid our annual visit to Donald, Mickey,
and Goofy at Disneyland. Then we swam a
bit more.

Luke was all right, too. Mum and Dad
accepted his presence almost as if he had
always been part of the family. Dad, who is
not exactly a sports fan, tried to talk to him
about waves and currents. Now and then I
would catch Mum sneaking glances at the
happy young couple in a way that suggested
that, truly and honestly, she was pleased
that her only daughter was now hanging
out with a surfer.

As for me, I acted my normal, mellow
self but, inside me, those old restless feelings were churning away once more. I
began to wonder why it was all right for
Amy to bring her boyfriend on a family

holiday while, if I mentioned taking a friend—Gip, say—it would be nervous breakdowns all round. I started thinking about my family—how what was normal and good so often became confused with what was odd and suffocating. Sometimes, when I looked at Mum, Dad, Amy, and Luke together, the image of Gip in my house crept up on me. I heard his voice, "Your life, man."

I tried to concentrate on the holiday but there was no escaping these thoughts.

One afternoon, we were lying by the pool, just Luke and me. Amy and Mum were shopping for presents, Dad was working in his room.

"So what d'you think of the family then?" I asked.

Luke looked up slowly from one of the many surfer magazines that were the only thing he ever read. The question seemed to take some time to be processed through his brain. He gazed across the pool, working out an answer to this question.

"Cool," he said finally.

I waited for something a little more detailed but Luke turned back to his magazine. He frowned slightly, either because the description of a particular wave was kind of hard for him to grasp or maybe to discourage me from any more tricky questions.

"So you think my dad is cool," I said in an irritatingly chirpy voice.

Luke kept reading. "Yeah."

"What do you think is particularly cool about him? The way he lowers his glasses and says, 'Magic word?' His new knee-length Bermuda shorts?"

"Not that kind of cool." He spoke levelly as if there was another kind of cool that a kid of my age wouldn't be able to understand. "I just meant that your dad is one of the good guys."

"My mum and dad have never even had a row."

Surfer-Boy laid down his magazine and closed his eyes wearily.

"Never ever," I said. "Kind of unusual, isn't it? Not a cross word between them. Ever. And I can't even remember them ever raising their voice to me or Amy. It was all smiles or seriousness, family games or little outings. I guess I can be pretty annoying sometimes—"

"Too right."

"But, even when I leave my room in a mess or get into trouble at school or hang out with my friend Gip—who my parents hate—they never lose control. They just look at me, kind of puzzled and slightly disappointed."

"Let me get this right." Luke gazed at me through half-closed eyelids. "You're complaining because your parents don't bawl you out?"

"Yeah, right, exactly. That's what parents are for, isn't it?"

Luke gave a great sigh. "There was this dude," he said. "A rock star. Rich. Talented. Successful. Everybody loved him. One day he told the newspapers that he was going to see a shrink—some psychiatrist guy. What for? Because everything was just too goddam great in his life. It spooked him out. He called it 'the Paradise Syndrome.'"

It took me a moment to recover from the shock of hearing Surfer-Boy say something that was almost interesting. "You think that's what I've got?" I asked. "Paradise Syndrome? Like this . . . dude?"

"I do, Tom. Don't knock the good guys. If it ain't broke, don't fix it."

I smiled at him, hoping that maybe he would come out with one or two more choice items from the Bumper Book of Completely Pathetic Clichés. The grass is always greener, maybe. Or the one about every cloud having a silver lining.

"I guess that's very true," I said in my most serious voice.

Luke was all talked out. He held the magazine in front of his face.

"How about your folks?" I asked. "What are they like?"

"Cool," he said.

I lay there for a few moments, thinking about what a sad mess of a person I was to be living in Paradise, yet wanting to spoil it all, about how, even though I loved my parents, I seemed to want them to be different from the way they were.

"I'll be in my room," I said, standing up.

I walked into the hotel. When I picked up my key from the foyer, the guy behind the desk surprised me by giving me an envelope. "You seeing your father?" he asked.

"Sure." I took the envelope. "I'll give it to him."

In the lift, I glanced down. Above my father's name on the envelope in the top left-hand corner were printed, in smart, ornate letters, the words "The Seraph Organization."

Then I noticed something else. The envelope was not sealed.

On any other day, it would not even have occurred to me to open a private envelope, addressed to my dad. I would never have dreamed of reading the letter inside.

But this was not any other day. This was now and I was upset. When I reached my room, I opened the envelope and, after a moment's hesitation, unfolded it, and read the letter that would change my life.

Dear Mr. Wisdom,

We are glad to confirm that you will both be visiting the factory for your annual de-brief and reconfiguration service on Wednesday, August 13, at noon. Your direct transport to Seraph will leave at 10:30 A.M. You will be

free to leave at 5 P.M. Your visitation code this year is:
OOPSPIZ352TYO.
We look forward to seeing you.

S. di Luca
Head of Reconfiguration Services

It seemed kind of odd—not exactly the sort of letter the boss of a food development company would send to one of its employees.

Something else. At the head of the letter there was no postal or e-mail address, telephone or fax number, simply the word **SERAPH**, written in bold letters.

I shivered, wishing now that my nosiness had not got the better of me. I put the letter back in its envelope but then, thinking of what Gip would do, I took it out again and made a note on the pad by the telephone of the code-number mentioned by S. di Luca, Head of Reconfiguration Services.

Then I sealed up the envelope and took it along to my father's room.

The large dining-room at the Excelsior is about the most soulless place you could ever eat dinner at. At one end is the self-serve buffet. At the other is some kind of Latin American band, all banjos, maracas, and fake cheesy grins. Between them, guests eat their meals under the watchful eyes of waiters who swoop down to take away plates within seconds of your finishing. So you join in, grab your food, get it down you as quick as possible and scram. It is big and comfortable and efficient, the Excelsior, but it just doesn't do atmosphere.

Yet there was an atmosphere at our table that night. At

first I thought that my dad had somehow sensed that I had been reading his private mail, but as the meal went on, it became obvious—to my amazement—that it was not me that was in trouble but my sweet angelic sister Amy and Old Chatterbox, her boyfriend.

There were looks across the table, silences. Amy and Luke behaved as if they were feeling guilty about something. Once or twice Surfer-Boy did that narrow-eyed, gum-chewing thing that bad film actors do to show how tough they are deep down. Amy was all flustered. She made stupid small talk, now and then laughing unconvincingly at her own feeble jokes. Mum was unusually silent.

In fact, it was only when we reached the ice cream stage of the meal that I began to understand the problem.

"Thomas, Wednesday." My father spoke as if he had suddenly remembered some minor bit of information he had almost forgotten to tell me. "Mum and I have to take our little business trip, as usual."

I smiled innocently. "Oh yeah, right."

"We were worried about what you would do with yourself."

I glanced at Amy. "We'll go to the beach, hang out, do the usual stuff."

Unusually, it was Luke who replied.

"Thing is, Tom, I got an appointment with some waves up the coast. There's a surfing competition at Ventura Beach. A few of the guys are going to be there. No way can I miss out—it's a whole day thing."

"Of course, the answer would be for your sister to stay here," said my mother. "But she seems to have decided that being with Luke matters more than helping out her parents just for once."

Amy pursed her lips and looked down at her plate.

"Excuse me," I said. "You all seem to have forgotten something. I'm twelve years old. I don't actually need a nanny, thank you very much. I'll be fine all by myself. Was that what all this fuss was about?"

"You should be grateful that everyone's so concerned about your welfare," said Amy, once more back in big-sister mode.

"Yeah, right. I'm really grateful. Next time I need my nappies changed, I'll let you know."

"And there's absolutely no need to be vulgar," said my father.

Mum laid a hand on mine. "We'll catch the train soon after ten and we'll be back before dinner."

"I'll see you off if you like." The words had left my mouth before I had even thought of them. "I love stations."

I looked across at Amy. Normally she would have been the first to laugh at the idea of her little brother being some kind of sad trainspotter but, right now, she smiled as if my new enthusiasm for railway stations was the most natural thing in the world.

In fact, they all seemed more relaxed around the table—relieved that I had cleared up this big crisis by letting them all go to their meeting or surfing competitions without bursting into tears.

At the time, it all seemed so normal.

8 · STALKING

I HAD NEVER DONE ANYTHING like this before. I tried a cigarette once, bunked off school a couple of afternoons. When I was younger, I went through a phase of nicking sweets and packets of chewing-gum from shops but this was different. It was a plan, a calculated act of rebellion. For once in his life, Thomas Wisdom—the kind of boy that other parents would point out to their children and say, "Why can't you be more like that nice Thomas?"—was going to do something completely, wildly unpredictable. Something wrong.

Why did I want to follow my parents? I've asked myself that question almost every day since I took that fateful journey to Santa Barbara Train Station. The answer dated back to my conversation with Gip in the park earlier that summer. All logic, common sense and brains told me that Gip's spy theory was like the guy himself—strange, interesting, but basically out of whack.

Yet something else, an instinct, a feeling in my guts, niggled at me day and night. I sensed that, beneath the normality of everyday life, there was a secret at the heart of the Wisdom family.

Maybe it was crazy, paranoiac, but, one way or another, I had to lay the thing to rest.

So I became a spy.

It may have been my imagination but, as we took the fifteen-minute walk to the station that morning, my parents seemed unusually tense, less conversational than usual.

"I never knew you were interested in trains," my mother said at one point.

"Not trains, stations. I'm just interested in the way they look. And I've never been to an American station before."

My father, who had been walking ahead of us, turned and smiled vaguely. "Maybe you'll be an architect, old boy," he said.

"My son, the architect," said Mum, trying the idea on for size.

"Yeah," I said. "Yeah, right."

So when we reached the station, I suddenly had to be the architecture geek, gawping at the plain building with its really interesting platform, fascinating ticket office and unusual waiting-room as if I was being given this great treat.

In line with my new enthusiasm, I was even able to ask my dad which platform their train would be leaving from and where they were heading.

A brief flicker of alarm seemed to cross his face. "We're on the other side of the tracks," he said. "We had better say goodbye to you here, old boy."

My mother kissed me and told me to go straight back to the hotel. I walked through the bright station arches towards the car park, pausing once to wave at them. They stood together, waved, then turned back into the station and out of sight.

I made my way around the car park, then ducked back into the main waiting area. I took the underpass that led under the tracks to the platform on the far side. Cautiously, I climbed the stairs slowly and looked around me.

The platform was deserted except for a small, gray-haired man in an Amtrak uniform who stood looking down the tracks as if that was his only job.

I asked him when the next train to Seraph was due.

"Seraph City?" He shook his head. "Ain't no trains go direct to Seraph from here. You'd best go to LA and change there." He pointed across the tracks. "There'll be one coming along in a couple of minutes on Platform One."

"Is there another platform on this side?"

The man looked at me suspiciously. "Just the one you're standing on," he said.

I wandered towards the underpass, confused. Where had my parents disappeared to? And, if they had to change trains to reach Seraph, why had the note I read specifically mentioned "direct transport"?

I was about to give up on the spying game when I became aware that, trotting up the steps towards me, was a young businesswoman with a briefcase in her hand. She must have thought I was staring at her because, as she passed me, she held my eye briefly before making her way down the platform and pushing her way through a small swing-door.

On an impulse, I followed. The door led into another underpass, about 100 yards long, at the end of which stairs led upwards to another door. Without looking behind her, the businesswoman led me into the daylight beyond.

We seemed to have emerged in an area behind the station where there was a small, covered siding.

Ahead of us was the strangest train I had ever seen. A low, squat machine consisting of one gray carriage and with a long strip of darkened glass stretching the length of it, like a stain, it looked more like a missile or a submarine than any kind of land transport.

My watch showed 10:26. The woman stepped through an open door at the back of the carriage. I had seconds in which to decide whether this was the train my parents were catching. I knew that I had gone too far to turn back. With a confidence that I wasn't feeling, I walked quickly towards the heavy door and stepped up onto the train.

The interior of the carriage was brightly lit but strangely silent with all the passenger seats facing away from where I stood towards the front of the train. Although it was almost full now, no one chatted or busied themselves in the normal way of people at the beginning of a journey. They all sat there, silently, patiently.

There was a spare seat by a nearby window. I slunk into it, turning my face to the darkened pane, praying that I had made the right decision and that, somewhere in the train, were my parents.

Two minutes passed. Three. Four. A middle-aged man in a dark suit who had arrived with seconds to spare, slipped into the seat beside me without even glancing in my direction. The train gave a sort of sigh and began to glide forward soundlessly.

I gazed out of the window while the train gathered speed. Then, as the center of the town gave way to the suburbs, I dared to look around me at my fellow passengers.

There was something calm and orderly about these people, almost as if they knew each other so well that any kind of conversation was unnecessary. The man beside me smiled briefly in acknowledgment of my presence and then relaxed into the sort of trance I had seen on the face of commuters back in London. As I looked about, I noticed that there were no children in the carriage. It occurred to me that perhaps this was some kind of business train for employees of the Seraph Organization but, if that was the case, it seemed odd that no one seemed surprised or curious that I was on board.

I was peering forward, trying to catch a glimpse of Mum or Dad, when I saw something that made my stomach lurch. Two rows ahead of me, there was the cropped, sandy hair and broad shoulders that I knew well. Moving slightly to my left, I could see the back of the head of his companion. Medium-length blonde hair.

There was no mistaking it. I was within a few yards of Amy and her lover-boy, Luke.

Crazily, I thought for a moment that I had stepped onto the wrong train and that we were heading for Ventura Beach before realizing that none of the other passengers seemed the type to be going to the seaside.

More afraid than ever of discovery, I huddled down in my seat and stared out of the window. I thought of the row at dinner last night and realized that it must have been a little invented playlet in which Dad, Mum, Amy, and Luke had been acting out parts for their audience of one. Were they all spies? What was it with me that excluded me from this family outing? Suddenly I felt alone and scared and angry. Maybe I was doing the wrong thing, stalking my own parents, but what was that compared to their deception of me? If they lied about today, what else was invented? Nothing seemed secure anymore.

For an hour or so, the train traveled silently through the

baked, scrubby terrain of rock and sand and sagebrush and cactus, interrupted occasionally by little groups of houses standing like frontier settlements. Not once did any of the passengers look at the scenery outside as they sat in blank-eyed silence in the carriage. It was as if they were on their way to something so important, so momentous, that the normal, everyday business of talking and looking about them had mysteriously been suspended.

The train began to slow. Outside, there were giant bill-boards by the track, advertising beer and jeans. One showed a fat, bald man surrounded by gleaming cars. *We're Going Price-Crazy at Bargain Bob's, Seraph City's Premier Used-Car Dealer,* it read. Sure enough, we appeared to be approaching Seraph but, to my surprise, no one in the carriage made a move.

We glided past some passengers on the platform who stared at our strange gray ghost train, away from the station and out of the town into a wilder, more desolate desert. There were few buildings to be seen now. The only sign of life was the occasional truck or car making its way down a distant, single-track road across the desert.

We must have traveled another five miles or so before I became aware that the people around me were stirring, picking up their bags and briefcases, glancing at their watches. The train slowed almost to walking pace. With a sigh, it entered what seemed to be a kind of tunnel, then drew to a halt.

The passengers stood up and made their way, still in silence, towards the front of the carriage where there was another exit. Amy and Luke were among the first to move and, as I watched them making their way forward, I caught a glimpse of my father a few rows forward, then, beside him, my mother. The gang was all here.

I waited in my seat until the carriage was almost empty. I stood up and walked down the aisle, the last passenger on the train. I stepped down. I saw a group of people making their way down the kind of brightly lit tunnel you might find between terminals at an airport. Fifty yards ahead, daylight shone through an open door.

When I emerged into the dazzling desert landscape, the brightness hurt my eyes. I looked around me. There was no sign of human habitation—no road or building and certainly no factory. Ahead of me I saw the passengers were walking across some open scrubland, an orderly file of people, each carrying a briefcase. I was entirely exposed now, a figure standing alone in front of the tunnel, but no one looked back. They kept walking across the stony sand, staring straight ahead of them, almost as if they were in a dream.

Then I saw where the passengers were heading. A small concrete building, like some kind of defense bunker or an electricity generator, stood in isolation. No tracks led to it and there were no windows in its bright, nondescript walls, so that it seemed almost invisible, part of the scenery around it, almost as if it had grown out of the landscape itself.

As I watched, the group of people carrying briefcases seemed to be forming an orderly queue at the dark green door. Because the line stretched away from me, I was unable to see what was happening at the front of the queue but, over the next few minutes, the number of people outside the hut seemed to get fewer and fewer. At one point, I darted further down the track to get a better view.

My parents and Amy and Luke were gone. Slowly, one by one, the passengers were being let inside the building, absorbed into its tiny space as if some conjuring trick were being performed.

It was only when there were about ten figures left outside that I could see what was happening. As the next man reached the door, he extended his hand to some button or panel. A few seconds later, the green door rose vertically. The man stepped forward into the darkness. The door descended.

I felt scared. The third to last person, a youngish woman, disappeared into the building, then the second to last, leaving one man, a young guy in his late teens. He made precisely the same movements as the others, the door rose—and suddenly I was alone in a deserted, silent landscape.

Apart from the strangeness of a hut, miles away from anywhere, that could make 100 or so humans disappear, there had been something almost ghostly about what I had just seen—the way they all walked, staring fixedly ahead of them, unspeaking, the queue they formed as if standing in a row outside a tiny hut by a deserted railway line was the most natural thing in the world.

I stood up and made my way slowly across the wasteland. When I reached it, I found that the bunker was even smaller than I had imagined.

It had occurred to me that, if Gip had been right and this was some kind of CIA hideout, there would be a defense mechanism or spy camera in place but the only feature on the concrete block was its dark green front door.

As I had seen my parents and their fellow-passengers do, I stood before the door and held out my left hand towards the patch of wall to the side of it. I touched the rough surface. With the faintest of clicks, a small square in the wall slid across, revealing a square pad—numbers on one side, letters on the other—glowing phosphorescently.

A number. A key. It was like de-activating a burglar

alarm. I remembered the letter that had been sent to my father and reached into the back pocket of my jeans. There, on the hotel notepaper was what Seraph's S. di Luca had described as my parents' "visitation code."

I took a deep breath, then slowly entered the code: OOPSPIZ352TYO. As I touched the final letter, the door began to rise. I was staring into a small, white room.

I stepped through the door.

9 · HOME

I WAS IN A SMALL, brightly lit room. I looked around me and saw that there was no exit of any kind. Even the door behind me seemed to have mysteriously become a solid white wall. I was in a tiny, box-like prison.

The lights began to dim. Within seconds, I found myself in total darkness. I heard a faint click and suddenly the floor seemed to fall away from me. As the room descended into the earth at a terrifying speed, I crouched on the floor, eyes tight shut, groping for something—anything—to hold on to.

How long did I fall? Thirty seconds? A minute? Whatever it was, it felt like a lifetime before I felt the floor beneath pressing into my hands and knees as the tiny chamber soundlessly came to a halt.

It was several seconds before I dared to open my eyes. When I did, I was startled to see that the darkness around me seemed to have changed in quality and was now a strange, glowing purple color unlike anything I had seen before. The air had changed, becoming heavy and warm with a faint scent of sulfur. Beyond the sound of my own breath, I heard a ghostly chorus of sounds, a discordant, metallic music, which seemed almost like unearthly voices communicating with one another.

"Mum? Dad?" I spoke the words, I know I did, but all that came from me was a whisper that was lost in the clamor around me.

I could see nothing through the thick, purple murk. I reached out to touch the wall to my left but my hand found nothing. I edged my way forward and groped around me—that wall had gone too. The very room in which I had descended had faded into nothingness.

It was warm but I was trembling uncontrollably. After a minute or so, I stood up—slowly, unsteadily, like a one-year-old about to take his first step—and, at that moment, something passed in front of me brushing my cheek like a warm breeze.

The terror that had been gathering within me surged up like nausea. I screamed, again and again, until my throat burnt, my jaw ached from the effort. Yet it was as if I was trapped in a nightmare, alone, unheard, the sound that was coming from me no more than a helpless, strangled gasp.

I had to move. Both hands outstretched before me, I took a step forward, then another. My legs felt stronger now. The warmth was less oppressive. It seemed to me that, all around me, there were invisible presences in the haze but that, mysteriously, they were not hostile. They were talking to me, calming me, taking me forward. As I moved forward, it was almost as if, with every step, I was becoming not only closer to them, but part of them.

Ten paces, twenty. The purpleness seemed to stretch to

infinity yet I found that I was breathing more easily. My terror was ebbing away. The nagging voice of normality that, seconds ago, had questioned what was happening to me, where I was, how I was going to return to reality, was receding, becoming distant and irrelevant.

Forty paces, fifty. I felt more powerful now, more my true self. I knew that I was walking towards wisdom, maturity, understanding—towards salvation. I was among friends. I had returned home after a long journey—not to the normal kitchen-and-telly home but a real home, a place of utter safety, a home of the heart.

I walked onwards in the gloom, knowing that wherever I went, I would be taken care of. The outside world suddenly seemed trivial and pointless. This was the only reality that mattered. The past—the whole of my life until now—had been a sort of restless, frantic dream from which I had now awoken. If one of the strange presences I felt all around me had told me, in an easy, friendly whisper, that I could stay here forever, I would have smiled and agreed.

I lost all track of time and place but at some point I stopped, somehow knowing that I had reached my destination. I looked down. The ground beneath my feet had developed gentle lines and markings in a light green, glowing color, as if I were walking across some kind of illuminated map.

They drew me inwards, closer to them. Without quite knowing what I was doing, I slowly crouched, then knelt, my hands reaching out to the contours around me.

Now, with the perfect logic of a dream, I saw that the landscape of which I was a part was actually moving, breathing gently, part of one great, living organism. I closed my eyes for a moment. When I opened them, I knew that what I had taken to be lines and contours were alive too. They were human bodies, lying flat upon their backs, naked, palms upwards, eyes open, smiling, as far as the eye could see. They were men and woman of all ages and shapes and yet they seemed unified by the same tranquil, blonde beauty.

I was not afraid or embarrassed. I knew in my soul that these people were more at ease with themselves than I had ever been. In fact, I was only aware of one overpowering emotion. I wanted to be like them. I wanted to be one of them.

Surprised by this thought, I gazed at the figure who was nearest to me. It was a woman—light-haired, handsome, friendly—and, although her features were unclear, I knew who she was.

"Hi, Mum," I said.

The sound that came from me was just a sort of sigh. My mother smiled in a way that I had never seen her smile before. I looked beyond her to see my father whose eyes were turned towards me.

Neither of them spoke. Yet, in my head, I heard their voices speaking in unison with complete clarity.

"Well done, Thomas," they said. "Go home now. We shall follow later."

I closed my eyes and was surprised to feel tears rolling down my cheeks. I turned back from the landscape of naked beings and started walking back in the direction from which I had come.

After a minute or so, I saw before me about ten people, fully clothed, carrying briefcases in a line. I joined them, walking slowly. At the front of the queue, each of them stepped forward into the purple darkness. There was a gentle swish of a door and they disappeared.

When it was my turn, I stepped forward too. Soon I was

ascending. Doors opened behind me and I was dazzled by the light of the Californian sun.

I swayed, almost lost consciousness. My eyes ached from the brightness and I buried my face in my hands. At that moment, I wanted, more than anything in my life, to return to that underworld where everything was perfect, where love was in every breath and the sharp, scratchy reality of life above ground had no place.

Someone laid a hand upon my shoulder. I looked up to see the woman I had first followed on to the train, it seemed like a lifetime ago.

"It's all right, Thomas," she said softly. "It is time to re-enter the world."

"But I don't want to."

"I know. I understand." She smiled kindly and began to walk slowly towards the tunnel where the train was waiting for us.

Casting a single glance behind me at the small bunker that contained such secrets and joy, I followed her.

10 · SAGEBRUSH

I REMEMBER NOTHING of the journey back to the hotel. One moment, I was in the California wilderness, standing beside a track with a group of smiling strangers, the next I was back in my hotel room, lying, fully clothed, on my bed. There was a telephone ringing. Blearily, I picked it up.

"Where are you, Thomas?" It was the voice of my sister, sounding unusually bright and bouncy. "We're waiting for you in the dining-room."

I looked at my watch. It was past seven o'clock in the evening. The way I felt—heavy-limbed and spaced out—it might have been seven in the morning after a night without sleep. Within my head, I could hear muffled sounds that were both strange and yet oddly familiar to me.

"Thomas?" Amy's voice crashed into the foreground. "Are you all right?"

"Yeah." I sat up. "I fell asleep. I was feeling kind of bushed. I'll be right down."

I hung up and tottered into the bathroom. The sounds in my head were growing quieter now, becoming like waves on a distant shoreline. I stared in the mirror and, for the briefest of moments, I had the sensation that I was looking into the face of a stranger. The features were the same, if a little paler than normal, but there was something about my eyes that seemed different.

Seraph. The events of the day came back to me with crazy clarity, the upside-down logic of a dream. I was back in the hut, the lift, the lowering of light to a purple haze, the lines of glowing bodies, the faces of my parents staring up at me, welcoming and questioning as if they were expecting something of me.

If it had all been a dream, I wondered where it had started. I was certain that I had gone to the station with Mum and Dad. If I had returned to the hotel having seen them off, surely I would have remembered the journey back.

My head drooped and I closed my eyes for a few seconds. I needed to think logically. There was a reason for this fantasy, I told myself. I had become obsessed by the idea that my parents had some kind of secret life. My sleeping brain had done the rest. Now all I needed was a sign, the smallest hint of evidence, that would prove that I had been in the hotel room that afternoon.

I breathed in deeply several times, then opened my eyes. I was staring down at my trainers. Caught beneath the laces was a sprig of greenery. I picked it out and stared at it as the truth began to dawn on me. It was sagebrush—wild, scrubland sagebrush.

I groaned in despair. I had my sign.

I took the lift to the ground floor and walked to the dining-room where I stood at the door, looking for my family and Luke. Then I saw them. They were sitting at a table near the window, laughing and talking among themselves as if nothing had happened. Behind them, the sun was going down over a still, glassy sea and, for a few seconds, as I watched, it seemed as if the four of them emanated a sort of glow that set them apart from the rest of the room.

Then Dad spotted me and waved me over.

I took my seat. There were jokes about how much I slept these days. Mum asked me how my day had been.

I stared at her for a moment. She knew how my day had been. They all knew. Rage flared within me, then, for reasons I didn't understand, suddenly died. "It was good," I said. "Yours?"

"It was fine," said Mum.

"Pretty much the usual," said Dad.

There was a silence and they all looked at me, almost daring me to ask more questions.

"How was the surfing?" I asked Luke.

Surfer-Boy winked in that irritating way of his. "Cool," he said.

"So everything's cool," I said. There were smiles around the table. Each of them seemed strangely energized and bright that evening, making me feel like a pale outsider. We each knew what had happened that day yet none of us, I now realized, was going to speak about it. There was some kind of mysterious game going on and, for reasons that I was unable to understand, I was playing along with it.

Mum seemed to sense what was going through my mind. She leaned forward and laid a hand on my arm. The smile on her face reminded me distantly of the look she had given me in the purple underworld of Seraph. "We can all relax and enjoy the rest of the holiday," she said. "Together and happy."

"Yeah." I moved my arm away. "Just the five of us."

My father looked up from the wine-list. "Not quite," he said. "As it happens, Cy Gabriel, the guy who heads up our department at Seraph, may be joining us on the night before we return. He's in town for a meeting. If no one objects, I was going to ask him along for dinner."

"Fine," said Amy.

"Sounds cool to me," said Surfer-Boy.

My father had not taken his eyes off me. "How about you, old boy?" he asked quietly.

I shrugged. "Supercool," I said.

11 · CY

WE ATE. WE DRANK. We laughed. We talked.
We swam. We sat under parasols and stared
out to sea. It was Santa Barbara as usual.
Sometimes for minutes at a time, I managed to forget what I had seen that afternoon on the prairie.

In fact, from the way my parents
behaved, I might have believed that it was
all some kind of dream. They ignored my
silences, my regular hints that I knew something about their secret lives. If anything,
they seemed more at ease than usual.
Sometimes I would catch them gazing at
Amy and Luke, or at me, with a sort of
goofy, contented smile that I found plain
embarrassing.

Forget it, I would tell myself. You saw
nothing. The sun was playing tricks on your
imagination. Then, once or twice a day I
would open the drawer beside my bed and
take out the Gideon Bible. There, between
its crisp white pages was a sprig of sage-

brush. I knew that I had really seen what I had seen, that it may have been completely inexplicable but that it had happened. And I knew, for certain, that what had happened that afternoon had changed my life forever.

I was not afraid during these moments. In fact, when I remembered those voices and allowed myself to be transported back into that other-worldly purple haze, I felt more content than I had ever felt before. Once I had felt childish. I had believed that no one really listened to me. Now I had the strange, inexplicable conviction that I had it within my power to grow, to achieve my true potential.

Yet there was something about this holiday—the fact that Mum and Dad were lying to me, the way Amy seemed to have removed her brain whenever Luke was around— that had begun to make me restless. Although I was not entirely thrilled by the idea of my parents' boss crashing our last night at the Excelsior, I was not heartbroken either. At least he was a new face.

He was late. While we all waited for him in the bar, Dad regaled us with stories from the life and times of Cy Gabriel—how Cy's fourteen-year-old son had crashed his Chevrolet into a water-trough on his ranch, how Cy had been out sailing in the bay when his boat tipped up and he had to be rescued because there was a shark alert, the day Cy had accidentally spilled a glass of water all over his finance director during some kind of heavy meeting. To tell the truth, he was beginning to sound like a big-time loser to me.

But when he turned up, Cy Gabriel turned out to be very different from the way I had imagined. He was probably about Dad's age but there was something bouncy and enthusiastic about him which made him seem younger. His car had had a blow-out on the highway, he said, and, even though he had kept us waiting for forty-five minutes, we were made to feel as if this latest crazy adventure of his made it all worth it.

To tell the truth, Cy Gabriel brought that last evening alive. He shook us all up with his energy and curiosity. Soon even Luke was joining in, telling tales of life on the ocean wave and revealing that he wanted to create a Web site for international surfers.

"What about you, Thomas?" Cy turned to me. "Have you thought of a career yet?"

"Architect, maybe," I said, thinking quickly.

"Wow," Cy smiled. "Any particular area?"

"I'm quite interested in railway stations." As I said the words, I realized that they sounded a touch unconvincing. "But I'd probably start with smaller stuff—bus stations, houses. I'm interested in small buildings as well. I saw something out of town—a little concrete bunker in the middle of the desert. Do you have any idea what that might be for?"

He looked at me evenly. "Some kind of communications thing, I'd guess," he said. "We're cabled up to our eyes in this country. Ever thought of going into your parents' line?"

It was my turn to smile. "I would if I knew what they did. They never exactly talk about their work."

"That's good. Husbands and wives who work together need to build boundaries between their different lives."

"What is food development anyway?"

"It's a great profession, Thomas. Not badly paid, loads of travel, great prospects. One thing's for sure—the world's always going to eat. Food development is where the future is."

I was kind of surprised by the way this conversation was going. Instead of being secretive, like my parents, Cy Gabriel seemed to be making some kind of sales pitch. I must have looked startled because Mum interrupted our conversation at this point. "Don't let yourself get brain-washed by this man," she said to me. "He's a great sales-man."

Cy held up both hands in surrender and, for the first time, I noticed a dark, red birthmark above his left wrist. "Only spreading the word," he said. "Just looking to save another soul."

"He's only twelve, Cy," said Amy and we all laughed, as if Cy had been a friend of the family for years.

The meal took its course and, explaining that he had a two-hour drive home, our guest said goodbye, shook hands with us all and, with many a promise that we would see each other next year, he made his way out of the door.

"What a great guy," said Amy, as soon as he had left. "That man is so nice."

"You seemed to be getting on well with him, Thomas," said my mother.

"He was all right," I said, suddenly anxious to be out of there and getting ready for bed. The truth was, I was sud-denly wishing I had spoken to him longer. I wished—for reasons I was unable to understand—that, instead of driv-ing to the airport the following morning, we were taking the freeway out to Cy's ranch.

"He comes over to England sometimes," said my father. "Maybe we'll fix up a Sunday lunch with him."

We made our way out of the dining-room. As we walked past the reception desk, the Spanish clerk called out, "Mr. Wisdom."

My father turned, but the clerk was holding out a piece of paper in my direction. "Other Mr. Wisdom," he smiled.

Puzzled, I took the paper. It was a message from the hotel receptionist.

It read, *Mr. Gip phoned. Please call tonight.*

"It's me."

There was a snuffling sound from the other end of the telephone and I imagined Gip in a tangle of whiffy bed-clothes. It would be four or five in the morning where he was, yet I knew that Gip wouldn't mind being woken. Time means nothing to him. Now and then he would read right through the night and catch up on his sleep in class.

"Hope I didn't wake your mum," I said.

"Nah. Nah. Nah." Gip made one of his usual animal noises. "She isn't around right now. How's old Santa Barbara, then?"

"It's good but . . . things have been kind of strange around here."

"Yeah?"

I was about to talk about my afternoon in the under-world but suddenly I felt reluctant to let Gip share my secret. The experience had been so personal that even mentioning it felt like a betrayal—not so much of my parents but of myself. "I'll tell you about it when I get back."

"It was the CIA, right?"

"Gip, what did you need to talk about? This is costing, man."

"Yeah, yeah. I got news about your dad's secret file. Old Rendle has decoded it."

"Oh, great." I felt surprisingly annoyed that our geek of a math teacher had not given the file back, as I had asked, but had gone through my father's private documents. I imagined Dad's reaction—not so much angry as disap-pointed—and thought of how he might have to tell Cy that secret company documents had been lifted by his own son.

Aware that Gip had gone a bit quiet, I muttered, "And?"

"He's flipping out big-time."

"That's news?"

"Nah, it's worse than usual. He won't talk to me about this file thing. He says it's private stuff."

I shook my head. "Why did you give it to him, you bozo? A teacher, of all people."

"You wanted my help." Gip stifled a yawn. "Call me when you get back. I'll give you his number."

"Maybe he'll just give me the file back and forget about it."

"He says he can't do that."

I swore and Gip actually laughed, as if spreading some of my family's most personal secrets around the neighborhood was some kind of little joke.

He was muttering some Gip-like encouragement about hanging loose or getting real or mellowing out but I was no longer in the mood. I hung up.

12 · BEAST

I SLEPT BADLY on the flight back home. Gazing out of the little circular window at the clouds below, I kept turning over in my mind the strange events that had occurred in California and wondering what lay in store for me back home. I cursed my own curiosity. Why had I talked to Gip about my family? What madness had led me to follow Mum and Dad into their own underworld? How was it that, of all people, Colin "The Beast" Rendle had become involved in my family crisis?

The Beast was not someone that you could imagine having a life outside school. It was rumored that he had once been a genius but had some kind of serious brain-box overload in his twenties and had decided to do something nice and easy with his life, a job that didn't require too much thinking. So he became a teacher.

Some would say that he never did recover from that crack-up. It was as if all the energy and genes in his body had gravitated to his massive brain, leaving nothing left for looks, shape, teeth, breath, conversation, or bodily hygiene. With his long, greasy hair, fluffy sideburns and manky brown corduroy suit, blotched and caked with ancient stains, he looked like a joke figure out of some cartoon.

There were school legends about the things that had happened to him in the past. One class had locked him in a cupboard for a whole lesson. Someone had stuck a Post-It message reading WEIRDO on the back of his jacket, where it had stayed until he returned to the staffroom at lunchtime. In one lesson, everyone had pretended not to be able to understand him. There was no end to stories about the Beast and year after year children had discovered new ways of making his life a misery.

If our class was not the worst, it was for one reason only: Gip Sanchez. From the first day Rendle had taught us, Gip seemed to bond with him in a way which none of us could understand. He sat at the front, ignoring the pandemonium all around him, making notes, listening full-on to every saliva-filled word, even laughing at the occasional lame joke that the Beast made. Sometimes, the two of them could be seen in the Beast's classroom in break-time or after school, chatting away, happy as a couple of hairy monsters could ever be.

And now, thanks to Gip Sanchez, the Beast was in control of a small part of my life. Wondering what on earth could have been on Dad's file which had caused Rendle to freak out, I drifted off into a fitful sleep.

The flight passed too quickly. On the way from the airport, we called in at the kennels where my dog suffered his usual nervous breakdown on being released from his prison, running around me in small circles, yapping, before rolling on to his back, whining ecstatically. When we reached the house, I took him out for a walk in the park.

Then, lagged out of my brain, I went to my room and lay on my bed.

Rendle could wait.

I must have been more tired than I had thought. One moment it was two in the afternoon, the next it was almost midnight. Mysteriously, I was in my pajamas now and my bag, which I had slung on the floor, had been unpacked.

I reached into the back pocket of my jeans for the slip of paper on which I had written Rendle's number, then padded downstairs to the sitting-room. It was time to call the Beast.

He picked up on the second ring.

"It's Thomas Wisdom, Mr. Rendle. Sorry for calling a bit late."

"Ah, yes . . . hmm, hmm." Sometimes, when Rendle's feeling particularly stressed, he makes this odd nasal grunt, like the sound a boxer might make while hitting a punch-bag. "Thomas . . . hmm, hmm. Good, yes."

"Gip said I should call. Gary Sanchez, that is."

"Right, well, of course, yes. But the fact is, Thomas, I need to talk to your parents about this . . . hmm, hmm . . . document."

"My parents." It was an alarmed squawk. I hesitated, listening for any sign of activity from upstairs before adding more quietly, "That's no good, Mr. Rendle. Didn't Gip explain the problem?"

"He said that you'd been playing around with your dad's computer and that your . . . hmm . . . curiosity got the better of you."

"It was a bit more than that."

"So can I talk to your mother now?"

"I'm afraid Mum's away for a few days. So is Dad, unfortunately."

"Hmm? Hmm?"

"Mr. Rendle, I think we should talk about this face-to-face. There are things I need to explain."

The Beast seemed to be having difficulty finding any words at all, so I jumped in quickly. "If you give me your address, I'll be there tomorrow," I said.

"Hmm, 7 Penrith Terrace, off the High Street but, Thomas—"

"I'll be there at ten tomorrow. Bye, Mr. Rendle."

I suspected that I would need company when I visited Rendle the next day, so I took Dougal with me on a lead. We arrived fifteen minutes early.

Rendle opened the door, looking unrecognizably normal in jeans and a white shirt. I stuttered my apologies for being early. "Nice dog," he said and gave a smile that was almost normal.

"Is it all right if I bring him in?"

"Of course." He waved us into the house and led us down a corridor into a neat sitting-room. I suppose I had been expecting the Beast to live in a bed-sit strewn with old papers and exercise books and unwashed coffee mugs because, as I stood there, he gave a little laugh.

"Bit more tidy than my room at school, eh?" he said.

I mumbled something polite.

"My mother keeps me in order," he said.

"Mother? I never knew—" I hesitated but there was no going back now. "I mean, I never thought you had a mother."

"She would have liked to meet you but she likes to have a lie-in during the morning."

I glanced around the room. Patterned carpet. Neat little

old-fashioned china dogs on the mantelpiece. A few silver-framed photographs on the dark wooden bookshelf. A writing-desk in the corner, on which a few papers were neatly stacked. It was not exactly what I had been expecting. "Just you two, is it?" I asked.

"Yes." Rendle ran a hand through his hair. "I'm an only child."

An awkward silence descended on the room as I tried, unsuccessfully, to imagine a childhood version of Rendle. "I've got a sister," I said.

"I know." He stood up suddenly. "Tea," he said. "Milk?"

I'm not exactly a tea person but I nodded. "Sounds good."

"What about the beast?"

I started in surprise before realizing that Rendle was looking down at Dougal. "Your dog," he said. "Does he need some water?"

"He's fine."

Rendle went into the next room and I heard him humming as he clattered about. Seeing him in this neat, little house, looking after his old mother, made me feel guilty about some of the things people at school had done to him.

It was so curiously relaxing in this house that, when Rendle returned, carrying two mugs, I was on the point of chatting to him a bit more, when he raised the question of my dad's file.

"Quite a little code on that document of yours," he said casually, as if it were some kind of tricky crossword puzzle. "It was unlike anything I've come across before—took me two days to crack it. I'll show you how I did it some time."

"That would be great. Can I have it back now? I'll just chuck it and forget this all happened."

Rendle shook his head slowly. "I wish we could do that,"

he said. "But, as I told you last night, I have to speak to your parents."

"I could give it to them for you. Save you the trouble." A note of desperation had entered my voice. "You can trust me."

"I trust you and Gary more than anyone else in your class but you've stumbled upon something that is very private. I considered destroying it but I don't think I can."

I sipped at my tea, playing for time. "Does it happen to have anything to do with national security?" I asked casually.

Rendle looked puzzled.

"Spies?" I asked.

He laughed. "No," he said. "It's more a personal matter." He paused. "You know, Thomas, you're very lucky to have such a wonderful family around you."

Almost as if she could hear these words, Rendle's mother began to call for him in a trembly, ancient voice from upstairs.

"Won't be a moment, Mother," he shouted without moving from his place.

She ignored him, calling his name again and again, sounding increasingly agitated.

Rendle stood up and suddenly he was his normal, battered self. "I won't be a . . . hmm, hmm . . . moment," he said. "My mother needs her . . . hmm, hmm . . . breakfast."

He had been out of the room for about a minute when an idea occurred to me. I wandered over to the desk in the corner and glanced at the papers that were on it. Under a single blank sheet, I found the numbered document that we had printed out from my father's computer. Attached to it was another typed sheet. I took a quick glance at the words at the top of the page.

Time froze. I stood there, unable to read anymore, unable to move. In the distance, I heard the voice of Rendle, talking to his mother upstairs. I lay the document back on the desk. I began to turn back into the room, to take my seat as if nothing had happened. Then, without giving myself time to think of the enormity of what I was doing, I grabbed the papers, called Dougal and slipped out to the hall. I glanced up the stairs, then silently let us out of the house. The door closed behind us with a quiet click.

I walked quickly down the street. Across the main road, there was a park where I found a bench. I sat down, lifted Dougal on to the seat beside me. I turned over the numbered sheet to stare at the version that Rendle had decoded. I looked at the headline again.

Taking a deep breath, I began to read.

The Adoption Papers of Baby Michael
Reference number: 0372AC19
Name: "Michael"
Date of Birth: 10/5/89
Place of Birth: Norwich and Norfolk Hospital, Norwich
Ethnic Origin: Caucasian
Mother: Karen Garnham
Father: Unknown

Social Worker's Report: Karen is eighteen years old and currently works part-time in a pub. She has had one previous child (Ref. No. 0372YG27) who was also put up for adoption. There have been no reports of medical or social problems with this child.

Karen is a healthy, good-hearted girl, but her background is unstable. She has two brothers and two sisters, all older. One brother is currently in a youth detention center and the other has also been in trouble with the police. One sister is married and living near Ipswich and the other is thought to be living in London. The Garnham family has always lived in the Holt area and is known to the local social services. All four children were on the At-Risk Register between 1968 and 1976. Karen's first child, a son, was put up for adoption in May 1986. The identity of Michael's father is unknown.

The implications of adoption have been fully explained to Karen who appears to have no doubt that it is the right course.

I am convinced that adoption is in the best interests of Baby Michael.

Health: Michael weighed 8 lbs. 6 oz. at birth. He has had no medical problems.

Character: Michael is a placid, easy-going baby who sleeps well. He has shown early signs of anxiety in the absence of his mother but is anticipated to settle well in his new home.

Proposed Adoptive Parents: Mark and Mary Wisdom.

Signed
Sally Rookyard
Social Services Department

I read the words on the sheet several times. Sensing that something was wrong, Dougal whined.

I stood up, folded the papers and slid them into my back pocket.

In a sort of trance, I began to walk slowly in the direction of my home.

13 · LIES

No, MY HEAD WAS NOT TEEMING with thoughts as I walked. No, I was not working out what exactly I should say to the people I had, until now, thought were my parents. I was numb. I felt sleepy. I wished I had never been saved from my life with Karen Garnham. In fact, right then, I wished I had never been born at all.

I reached home and went straight to my room where I lay down on the bed, turned my face to the wall and closed my eyes. I didn't cry but my eyes were full and I noticed that the pillow was damp. I wanted the world to go away.

Behind me, the door opened. I heard my mother's voice. She called my name twice, then walked over and gently shook my shoulder.

I turned over and, staring into her eyes, forced myself to remember that this was no longer the face of my mother.

"Go away," I said.

She looked shocked—more surprised than angry. "Are you ill?"

"Yes," I said.

Later, she brought me soup and a cake. I refused to talk to her. When I finished it, I placed the tray outside the door.

I couldn't sleep. My mind churned over and over with what I knew. I cursed Gip for his pathetic spy-obsession. I writhed with rage that stupid, snaggle-toothed Rendle had interfered in my life. I tried to understand what I had done to Mark and Mary Wisdom to deserve what they had done to me.

The house was silent when, at some early hour in the morning, I rose from my bed. I walked slowly down the corridor to the room where my adoptive parents were sleeping. Without a moment's hesitation, I pushed open the door and switched on the light. They lay in bed, blinking, looking afraid and strangely old.

"I want to leave home," I said.

At first they thought I was sleepwalking. As I stood there at the end of their bed, eyes blazing, hands trembling, as if I had come to murder them in their bed, my former mother huddled close to my former father.

"I think he's having a dream," she said. "Don't wake him, Mark. Sleepwalkers have to come around gradually."

"I'm not sleepwalking." I heard my voice screaming these words. "This is me. This is real. You remember real, don't you? From like before you started lying to me? Or is that so long ago that you've forgotten about it?"

Normally, when I get stressed out or upset it's Mum who takes control but now her face was as pale as the sheets of her bed.

"Perhaps it would be a good idea if you went to your room before you say something you might regret." My former father spoke in his business voice. At any other time, that cool, grown-up, nothing-can-faze-me tone might have stopped me in my tracks, but not tonight.

"What about you? Isn't there anything you've said that you might regret? Over the last twelve years, for example— since the tenth of May 1989. Can you think of one little thing you might have forgotten to tell me?"

My ex-parents glanced at one another. They knew what my problem was now.

"Thomas." The woman formerly known as "Mum" made to get out of bed but the expression on her face, the gentle soothing voice—it was all just another lie.

I swore. I swore and swore and swore and swore. I said words that I never knew I knew, things that I had heard kids using at school. Once I had felt sorry for them with their pathetic need to shock but at least they belonged some- where. At least their lives had not been one long, never- ending lie. At least they had families.

I was on my knees, swearing like a crazed madman, and the two people I had once trusted were each side of me, holding me, enveloping me in their arms, making soothing sounds, and I was fighting against them saying that I never wanted to see them again, that I wanted to go into a home where I belonged, asking why they hadn't left me where I belonged.

This weird, noisy wrestling-match must have continued for several minutes. Slowly, more out of exhaustion than anything else, I grew quiet. I was half-led, half-carried downstairs to the kitchen where I sat at the table between them. My former father placed a wine glass in front of me and told me to drink. The liquid burnt my throat and brought more tears to my eyes.

"Drink," he said. "You need it."

Feebly now, and with defeat in my voice, I swore once more. I took another gulp. My throat hurt but I welcomed the pain. So what if it made me ill? With a bit of luck, I would be sick all over their precious kitchen.

"We need to talk." My former father spoke gently and firmly. My former mother held my hand as if, at any moment, I might run from the kitchen, out of the house and into the darkness outside, never to be seen again.

There was silence for a moment. My head was swimming. The only sound I could hear was my own sobbing breaths.

"We were young and happy together. We had Amy. But we had been told that I couldn't have another baby." My former mother spoke quietly and deliberately, like someone who has been given a truth drug. "We talked about it, Dad and me. Amy was a lovely little thing but we had always dreamed of having a big family. Eventually, there seemed to be no choice. We weren't complete, the three of us. We were missing something in our lives. We put our names down at an agency. We were interviewed again and again. We were watched and studied for months. Everyone said that it was difficult to adopt a child. We had almost given up hope when we received word that something had gone wrong with a planned adoption, that there was a chance that our dreams might come true. A baby boy. Up in Norfolk."

"It was you, old boy," said my former father in a voice which I suppose he thought was full of love.

"You." My former mother squeezed my hand and gazed into my angry, wounded eyes. "We traveled up, the three of us. I can remember it as if it were yesterday. Amy had never been so excited. She chatted and laughed on the back seat of the car, asking every few minutes how much longer it would be. She was nine years old but the thought of having a baby brother was the best present she had ever been given. We were excited too, of course, but we were nervous—"

"Terrified," said my former father.

"What if you didn't like us? What if you looked up and screamed your little head off? Were we being fair on Amy? Would we be good enough parents for you? Thousands of couples wanted children. What made us think that we had the right to take over a life? But we got there. This woman met us, took us into an office and told us a bit about you—your mum, your background, how the couple who were to have adopted you had discovered something—not about you but about your would-be adoptive mother, a health thing—and all we could think of was what you were going to be like. All that drama you had caused in your short life. The woman led us into a room. There was a row of cots. A couple of the babies were crying. The room was all bright and colored and full of paintings and mobiles hanging from the ceiling but it was the saddest place I had ever been. We were led to the end cot and there you were, just lying there, a solemn little man staring up at us, more strangers there to cluck and chat over him. Amy leaned over the cot and touched your face. You took her finger with your left hand and you held on, your eyes looking into hers. She pretended to pull away but you held on. She laughed. You smiled. I cried. It was as if you had always belonged to us but had been waiting there all these months. It was the most perfect moment of my life. You were so beautiful."

"Yeah yeah," I muttered.

"They gave us your papers. We took you away in the carry-cot we had brought with us. They called you Michael but you somehow didn't look like a Michael. On the way back to London, we all decided on your name. Thomas. Thomas Wisdom."

I looked from one of them to the other. They both wore goofy, dazed half-smiles on their faces. I guess they expected me to burst into tears at this point, sob out words of gratitude that they had rescued me from the home, but my heart was stone.

"Year after year, we meant to tell you." My former father took up the story. "But we knew it would change everything. For the first five years, the agency kept in touch with me. They told us how important it was to explain to you where you came from. We would know the moment, they said. But the moment never came. When everything was good, we didn't want to spoil it. When it was more difficult, it seemed wrong to add to the difficulty."

"You know what?" I said. "I think you're still not telling me the truth."

My former father's head dropped, either from exhaustion or from shame. My former mother squeezed my hand more tightly.

"We're tired," she said. "We'll talk some more in the morning."

I went back to my room and lay on my bed. Although my limbs were aching as if I was coming down with a fever, my brain refused to close down for the night. It churned and turned and seethed with various hot, confused versions of what had happened to me over the previous hours. In a strange half-waking, half-dreaming state, I saw a procession of characters—my former parents, Rendle, Amy, my real mother, even Cy from California. They were caught up in some sort of game, a dance in which the person at the center of it all—little me—suddenly seemed utterly insignificant.

When I awoke, it was past nine. Briefly I had forgotten

what had happened, that I was no longer Thomas Wisdom from a neat street in suburbia, but Michael Garnham from wild and woolly Norfolk, but, within seconds, the truth came crashing in at me. I groaned, lay in bed for a moment, then sat up.

Normally at this time, Mr. and Mrs. Wisdom, my ex-parents, would have left for work but I heard them talking in low voices downstairs in the kitchen. As soon as I appeared, they would probably start at me again, giving me the new version of my life, telling me how I was more than a son to them because I was not actually their son, chucking in words like "belonging," "family," and "love"—above all, love—trying to rub away the past or make it into a pretty, fairy-tale picture.

I had had enough of it all. I needed to get some space between me and my former family's house. I crept to the bedroom and dialed the number of the one person in the world that I could trust.

Gip answered on the second ring.

"Meet me in the park," I said, and hung up.

14 · CHRISTMAS

GIP DOESN'T DO EMBARRASSMENT. Events—even big events like his mum moving out for a few weeks to live with some guy—seem to wash over him like a stream around a rock.

But that morning, when he arrived and found me sitting on our bench, he seemed almost worried. "You look rough," he said. "Tanned but rough." He offered me some chewing-gum.

As I took it, I noticed that my hand was shaking. He sat down beside me. Acting casual, he asked, "So how was Rendle?"

"He was OK."

"I rang him but he refused to tell me what happened. He kept saying you had run away from the house—that he needed to see you."

I looked across the park. Then, as casually I was able, I said, "He told me who I was." I stared Gip full in the face. "I'm adopted."

"Eh?" Gip gave an awkward, snickering

laugh as if I had made some kind of bad-taste joke. "You?"

"Me."

"But that's ridiculous. You look just like your parents. This must be some kind of mistake. Rendle's lost it."

I shook my head. Slowly, clearly, so that there could be no misunderstanding, I told him what had happened. Rendle. The file. Last night. The confession of my former parents. Now and then, Gip seemed about to ask a question but I needed to tell it all—every word that had been said, everything that I felt. I talked and talked and when I fell silent, Gip had nothing to say. He stared at me for a moment. His arm twitched as if he were about to reach out for me but he must have sensed that right now I didn't want to be touched. "Bummer," he said at last.

I smiled. Gip knew my secret—every foul, squalid, cheating little bit of it—but, now that it was out, nothing really changed. It was a bummer, but we were still Gip and Tom, sitting in the park, together. For the first time in twenty-four hours, it occurred to me that I might be strong enough to come through this thing without too many dents and scrapes and abrasions.

"Did you mean it about leaving home?" he asked.

I stared at the ground. "I've trusted them all my life," I said. "How can I go on living with them now that I know that everything was a lie? If they lied about that, what else were they lying about?" As I sat there, I remembered holidays, games in the garden, Christmases, parties, jokes, bedtime stories, breakfasts. Suddenly even my memories were a fraud.

"I could fix you up with a place to stay," Gip said suddenly. "Somewhere no one will find you."

I looked at him, surprised.

"I've got this room across town. It's a sort of hideaway I use when things get heavy at home."

I suppose I should have seen then how strange it was that Gip, at the age of twelve, had a second home but right then I could think of nothing but my own problem. "Thanks," I said. "But I've got to face this myself, head on."

"Colin Rendle wants to see you. He's panicking."

"Yeah." I laughed briefly. "What a heartbreaker that is."

"He might be able to help. He's the only person who knows about this."

"Help?" I shook my head. Was it really likely that a teacher so hopeless that he could be locked in a cupboard by his own class would be of any use whatsoever in a real crisis? But then I remembered the look on his face when I had seen him, the way he had called out to his mother.

"OK," I said, standing up. "Maybe it's worth a try."

Rendle was not exactly prepared for a visit. When he opened the door quickly and impatiently to see Gip and me standing there, it didn't take a genius to see that our timing had been kind of unfortunate. The sleeves of his shirt were rolled up. The V-necked patterned sweater that he liked to wear had little drops of water down the front. Flecks of soap were on his face and in his hair. He looked like the Mad Phantom of the Launderette.

"Thomas, Gary." He wiped his hands on the seat of his baggy brown corduroy trousers. "What a . . . hmm . . . surprise."

"Yeah, Colin, how you going?" Gip spoke to the teacher as if he were some kind of elder brother. "I found Thomas for you. We need some advice."

"Now?" Rendle winced. "Any chance of you coming back later?"

Gip gave a brief, shaggy nod in my direction. "It's kind of urgent."

"Hmm." The teacher turned, walked through the dark

hallway and into the sitting-room. "You'd better come in then."

We followed him inside, Gip first, then me, closing the front door behind us.

When we reached the sitting-room, we quickly became aware of the reason for Rendle's embarrassment. In an arm-chair, silhouetted against the net-curtained window, sat a gray, shriveled-up figure. As our eyes became accustomed to the light, we saw that she was a little old woman almost lost in a dark blue dressing-gown. Shining in the gloom were her two skinny legs, like white twigs. Her feet were in a plastic bowl, full of soapy water.

"These are my friends—Gary and Thomas." Rendle leaned over her and spoke in a loud, deliberate voice.

"Hi," said Gip.

"Hello," I said.

"Has Father Christmas been yet?" The old woman's voice was surprisingly clear.

We glanced at Rendle who smiled desperately.

Mrs. Rendle chuckled crazily. "You can tell me, boys," she said.

"Yeah." It was Gip who spoke first. "He has. Good old Santa. He was really generous too."

"He hasn't come to me. When you get old, he seems to forget all about you." Mrs. Rendle sighed and all the sorrows of the world seemed to be in her voice. She glanced contemptuously in the direction of her son. "He blocks the chimney, you know," she said.

"Mum, I don't think the boys should hear about that," said Rendle with a gentle despair in his voice that I had never heard before.

"He thinks I won't remember. Give the old bag a foot-wash and she'll forget all about Father Christmas—that's what he thinks." Mrs. Rendle made an odd clicking noise with her teeth then, without warning, said the worst swear word I've ever heard outside the school playground.

"Come on, Mother." Rendle smiled apologetically.

"I don't like Father Christmas anyway," said Gip quickly. "He always brings you exactly what you don't want. I wish he'd just give us all a break and . . . sugar off."

Rendle knelt down, lifted his mother's frail little feet, one by one, out of the bowl and dried them with neat, dabbing movements.

"He's a man; what can you expect?" said Rendle's mother. "Stop tickling me."

Rendle tenderly pulled down the old woman's nightdress and closed her dressing-gown. "Take a seat," he said. "I'll just take my mother upstairs."

Mrs. Rendle looked from Gip to me, then back again to Gip as if she had noticed that we were there for the first time. "Has Father Christmas been yet?" she asked.

"Mother." Rendle spoke more firmly. "Bedtime now." In one surprisingly graceful movement, he placed one arm beneath her legs, the other behind her back, and picked her up as easily as if she were a five-year-old child.

The old woman began to whimper. "Are you having a party?" she asked, looking up at her son. "Please, can I stay for the party? I promise to be good."

"We have to talk about something, Mother. Let's turn on the telly for you, upstairs. I think it's almost time for the weather-forecast." Murmuring quietly about areas of low-pressure, he left the room and made his way up the stairs, his mother in his arms.

"Lemme outta here," Gip muttered. We both laughed guiltily.

When Rendle reappeared, he had pulled down his

sleeves and wiped the soap off his face. He strode into the sitting-room with the fake authority he tried unsuccessfully to use at the beginning of a lesson at school.

"Sorry about that." He sat down but still seemed tense, as if ready to bound upstairs at any moment. "It's Christmas every day of the year in this house. Which is not as fun as you might think." Rendle sighed and stared ahead of him for a moment. Then he seemed to pull himself together. "And how is everything with Thomas?" He gave me a toothy smile.

"Fine," I replied automatically. Fact is, this little scene from the Beast's private life had made me forget my own problems for a moment. Now, with a lurch of the stomach, I remembered it all. "Actually, not fine at all," I said.

"You spoke to your parents."

"My ex-parents, yes. They told me where I came from. They said they had gone to this adoption agency, like it was some kind of pet shop for kids, and they picked me out and took me home. I think I'm meant to feel totally grateful to them, but I don't. I hate them."

"You're wrong, Thomas. I can see that—"

"I hate them and I'm moving out."

Rendle looked pale and unhappy. Somehow I could sense that he was not used to big family crises. His never-ending Christmas Day with his mother may have been difficult but at least it didn't require any decisions. He just had to wash her feet and keep her calm.

"I didn't know what to do," he said in a distant voice. "At first, all I could think of was solving the problem. I worked on the code for days. When I began to see how it worked, I laughed at the brilliance of it. I took some numbers in the middle of the file. It was a sentence about Karen Garnham. I thought it must be some kind of made-up story. Then I started from the beginning. It was a while before I began to understand what exactly it was that I was translating. By then it was too late to stop. When I got to the end, I agonized over whether I should pretend that the code had defeated me. But I thought you would take it to someone else. I tried to imagine how I would feel if I were you." His voice tapered off miserably.

"Thanks," I muttered. "I mean, really thanks. You were right. Twelve years of lies is enough."

"They're still your parents." Rendle spoke firmly. "I'm sure they love you as much as if they were your real mum and dad. Maybe more."

"Yeah, right."

"I've met them," said Rendle. "It's obvious that they care about you. They're good people—better than most of the parents I see."

I shook my head. "If you care for someone, you don't lie to them," I said.

"They thought it was for the best." There was a hint of desperation in Rendle's voice. "It was just one untruth. They probably thought that telling you about your real mother would upset the life they had made for you."

For some reason, a vision of my former parents lying naked in the haze of the sub-desert underworld entered my head. "It wasn't just one untruth," I said. "There are other lies—big lies—that they're not telling me about."

Gip and Rendle were looking at me but I was not in the mood to tell them more.

"What d'you think we should do, Colin?" Gip asked and, although I said nothing, I was grateful for that "we."

The teacher sighed. "Talk. Thomas has a lot of talking to do. He's got to try and understand the reasons for what happened."

"Yeah, right, understand. That's going to be easy," I said.

"The other question is what I should do." Rendle spoke more briskly now. "I have a professional problem in all this. For better or for worse, I have this knowledge about you— and you're a pupil. I really should talk to someone about it."

"Like who?" asked Gip.

"Like Mr. Dover—Mrs. Fredericks, maybe." He spoke the name of the headmaster and my class teacher with a sort of weariness.

"Won't they be on holiday?" Gip asked.

"There's an emergency number."

From upstairs could be heard the voice of his mother, calling his name. Rendle started like a child who has been caught doing something wrong. "Boys, I'd better see to my mother."

We stood up. "Mr. Rendle," I said. "I need to think about all this. Give me twenty-four hours. Promise you won't talk to anyone until we speak again."

He frowned, then nodded reluctantly. "So long as you don't do anything foolish. Stay at home. Talk to your . . . your folks. Try to understand." He laid a bony hand on my shoulder. "Right?"

"Right," I said.

"It's going to be OK."

"Somehow I don't think so," I said.

15 · EAST

THAT WAS THE DAY when I discovered that, whatever else was wrong in my life, I was lucky to have Gip Sanchez around—he was the best friend in the world.

He must have seen that I was kind of wasted by the time we left the weird, unhappy house of Mr. Rendle. In the past twenty-four hours, I had discovered that I was not who I'd always thought I was, I had faced up to the fact that my entire life had been a lie, I had spent a night of sleepless torment and then, just to round it all off, I had tiptoed through the wonky winter wonderland of the Beast's poor, Christmas-crazed mum.

I was in bad shape, and Gip took over.

"You've got to phone home," he said as we stood on the corner of the road where Rendle lived.

"Forget it," I muttered. "Home's not home anymore."

"OK, so you hate them right now but

there's no point in worrying them. Stay out too long and they'll go to the busies. Things are complicated enough, man."

My brain was working at half-speed and it took a few moments for me to realize that, when Gip referred to "the busies," he was talking about the police. "I don't care," I muttered.

"Call your folks," he said, taking a phone out of his pocket. He stopped beside it. "Either you do it, or I will."

There was something about Gip when he was in this mood that was so steely and strong that resistance was pointless. Somehow you knew that, whatever you were going through, he had survived worse. He had the power of a survivor.

He held the mobile phone out to me. "Your call, Tom," he said.

I dialed. Mum replied. She sounded kind of fraught. I told her not to worry about me. She asked me to come home. I said I had things to do. She started crying. I told her I would be back sometime. She asked me to promise I would return by nightfall. I hesitated. Suddenly everyone was asking me to make promises. I glanced at Gip, closed my eyes and sighed. I thought of my bed, my room. I nodded. She started talking again. "Yes, I said yes," I snapped. I hung up.

"Why am I always the person who has to behave?" I murmured.

Gip slung an arm round my shoulder and hugged me briefly. "Because you're Thomas Wisdom. That's the way you are. Now we're going to hit the town."

We took a bus, then another bus, then went by underground. We ended up in a part of town that I had never heard of, let alone visited. The streets were shadowy and litter-strewn and the windows of the shops were covered in wire mesh as if, at any moment, an invading army was going to swarm in, smashing and mugging and grabbing the few bits of manky food and tins that were on their shelves. About twenty yards above the road down which Gip led me was a giant motorway taking cars and lorries out of town. The rumble of engines and the swish of tires on tarmac seemed to come from another universe where there was color and money and hope, where people could escape from the gray, dingy world of city-dwellers.

We turned into a narrow street where a few wrecked cars seemed to have been dumped. The houses were big and solid and must have been elegant years ago but now the plaster was crumbling off them and most of their windows were boarded up.

"What is this place?" I asked, maybe a touch nervously.

"Home away from home." Gip smiled and it was true that he seemed more at ease than he usually was. His limp was almost a skip as he climbed the steps up to the last house on the right where all the windows were flung open and music could be heard from high up on the top floor. "This is where I come when things get heavy back at my place. It's a sort of refuge."

He took a key from his pocket and let himself into a hall where a big motorbike stood. Dark, gleaming bits of its engine lay on a greasy newspaper on the bare floorboards. Gip squeezed past it, kicking an empty beer can as he went, and made his way up the stairs.

"You rent a room here?" I asked in a low voice as I followed him.

He laughed. "Nobody rents here. The council's meant to be knocking the place down. In the meantime, it's a hangout for anyone who needs a roof over their heads."

"Like, a squat?"

"Something like that." Gip reached a bright open room on the first floor that had been painted in a wild, crazy, yellow color. A few cartoon-like pictures and graffiti had been scrawled on the walls but, although the spelling was dodgy—even the swear words looked wrong—there was nothing threatening about the place. In the far corner of the room, three people sprawled on the floor in front of a big, old-fashioned TV.

"Yo," said Gip, opening a fridge that was behind the door.

A girl with tangled dreadlocks and a lot of metalwork about her face glanced over her shoulder. "Gippy, where you been?" she said without any particular curiosity in her voice.

Gip was gazing into the moldy depths of the fridge. To my surprise, there was a six-pack of cola. He took two cans and handed one to me. He nodded in the direction of the door. "I'll show you my room," he said.

We went up another flight of stairs to a corridor with two closed doors on one side and one on the other. Gip walked to the last door, took out his keys, unlocked it and stood back to usher me in. "Welcome to the secret world of Gip Sanchez," he said.

The first thing I noticed when I stepped into the room was the noise. Within what seemed like a matter of yards from the low, small window, traffic was thundering by on the motorway flyover. Then I looked around me—it was like staring into Gip's soul. There were posters for computer games on one of the walls. In a corner lay a mattress with gray sheets and a few science fiction paperbacks scattered about on the floor. On a desk against the opposite wall was a laptop computer.

"Wow," I said quietly.

"Everything a guy could possibly need."

"But . . . how?"

"I was nine when I first stayed here. My mum had kicked me out for the weekend when she took up with some new guy. I met up with some kids in central London. This became the only place I could escape. I got a key cut. People come and go here but I kept my room."

"Where did the computer come from?"

Gip looked shifty. "That kind of fell off the back of a lorry. One of the other guys is good at hacking and stuff, so we can go on-line for free."

I walked over to the window and watched the stream of traffic—lorries and coaches and vans and cars with their drivers and passengers gazing ahead of them as if they were hypnotized. Now and then I caught sight of a child gazing blankly in our direction from a backseat. For them, I seemed to have become invisible. They belonged to a different universe—a place where people belonged together, where they knew where they were going.

"Quiet spot too," I said.

Gip laughed. "You should see it at rush hour."

"Where's the road heading?"

"Somewhere east, I guess."

There was an alcove underneath the window. I sat down and stared out at the traffic passing by. In spite of the roar and thump of the noise in the air, I felt at ease in this place. "Maybe I could stay for a while," I said.

Gip winced. "Not a good idea," he said. "We get a few hard cases hanging out now and then. It's not your sort of place."

"Thanks a bunch." I wasn't sure I liked this new Gip— all concerned and responsible and stopping me from doing things I wanted to do, almost as if he had become some kind of uncle or something.

Maybe he could tell the direction of my thoughts because he kicked my foot as if to tell me to snap out of it.

"So tell me what happened in the States," he said.

"I could use another Coke," I said.

An irritated look crossed Gip's face but he kept quiet. Then he shrugged and limped towards the door.

By the time he had returned with two more cans, I had made up my mind. It was true that Gip bore some responsibility for what had happened to me—in fact, it had been his crazy curiosity that set the whole thing in motion. The fact that he had kept this part of his life secret from me was none too thrilling, either. But, in the end, I had no one else to turn to.

Something within me resisted confiding any more in him but, at that moment, my defenses were down. I took a long swig of Coke.

"My parents went to a place called Seraph," I said. "And I followed them."

I told him everything. No matter how crazy and absurd, no matter how embarrassing, I spilled it all out. I told him I thought it might have all been a dream. I told him about the sprig of sagebrush. When I finished talking, I felt empty and desolate inside, like the biggest traitor who has ever lived.

Gip said nothing. He gave a long, disappointed sigh and stared out of the window.

"You don't believe me," I said. "I can tell. You think I've lost the plot." For reasons I couldn't understand, tears pricked my eyes. I found that my cheeks were wet.

"I believe you." He spoke sadly. "I believe every word you've spoken."

Our eyes locked for a long few seconds—not because it was some kind of gloopy buddy-moment, like in the movies, but because there was nothing left to say. He gave a shrug and a weird sort of grimace. "Here we go," he murmured under his breath.

It seemed a strange thing to say but then it was a strange moment. Later, I would remember that look and those words.

There was no turning back for either of us.

16 · WEST

I WENT HOME, BUT somehow it wasn't home anymore. As soon as I had said goodbye to Gip on the corner of my street and began walking towards the house where I had lived for all my life, I felt a lurch of anger in my stomach. In my mind, my home had been transformed into a prison with the people who had once been my parents as warders.

Twelve years ago they had collected me from where I really belonged, brought me back here as if I were some kind of thing, a family accessory, and had raised me, pretending for every second of every day and every night that I was theirs, not something that had been ripped from another place, other parents. I was not here because I belonged but because they needed a second child to make their precious lives complete. None of this was about me. I was just caught in the middle. In fact, I could have been another me, another spare child altogether, and it would have made no difference to Mr. and Mrs.Wisdom.

A prison, but one with a key. As I approached the house, I took the front-door key from my pocket. I slowed down as I reached the gate leading up our garden path, then walked on. The immaculate company car belonging to my former parents was parked, all smug and gleaming, on the other side of the road.

On an impulse, I crossed the road. I crouched down beyond the car and, without even bothering to check whether anyone was watching, drew the sharp edge of the key in my hand in great swooping strokes across the car's elegant, dark paintwork. The scratch sounded like a scream.

Feeling better, I stood up, walked across to the house and let myself in. I smiled when my former mother greeted me in the hall and, mistaking me for someone I used to be, she hugged me. I shook her off and told her I would be upstairs.

On the first floor, I hesitated. The door to my father's study was slightly open. I peered inside. The room was empty.

I sat down in his chair. Behind him was a rack filled with his precious classical music CDs. I glanced at them— Albinoni, Bach, Beethoven. They were, of course, in alphabetical order. I took the first on the rack and opened it. I took out my key again. Dad, dear Dad, would find a message where he least expected it.

I moved fast. I was like someone in a factory—grab, open, scratch, replace, again and again. I had reached Vivaldi by the time I heard footsteps on the stairs. I put back the last piece of my handiwork and, without even looking at my former mother, I went to my room and shut the door behind me.

I lay on my bed. I took the door-key out of my pocket. The end of it sparkled from the work it had done. I closed my eyes and remembered the magic, the power, I had felt as I made my mark.

I was me at last and no one was going to lie to me, pretend to me, patronize me ever again because I was a new person.

MG. I was MG. Michael Garnham. My mark was on the world and the world had better be ready for me.

I was expecting trouble. The two things in the world that were precious to my ex-father were his car and his music. But when I went down for supper that evening, I was in for a surprise. There was no sign of my former parents. Instead, casually reading a newspaper in the sitting-room, was Cy Gabriel.

"Thomas." He stood up as I walked in and shook my hand. "I've got a meeting tomorrow," he said. "Mark and Mary asked me over. I hope it's not inconvenient."

"Not really." I slumped into the chair opposite.

Cy laid down his paper. "So how you been doing?"

I tried for a smile but didn't make it. "I've been better as it happens."

There was silence in the room. At that moment, I wanted to confide in this man. Although he was virtually a stranger to me, he had the air of someone who had seen all kinds of stuff, who understood what it was like to be alone, confused, and lost.

As if he could read my mind, Cy said softly, "I know what happened, Thomas—I heard."

"I'm not Thomas."

Cy smiled. "Sure you are. You're the same smart guy you were when I met you in Santa Barbara. You've found out something about your past. That doesn't change who you are. Thomas Wisdom just got a bit more wisdom."

I looked out of the window. It was true that, however hard I tried, I was never going to be Michael Garnham.

"Your parents must have been crazy not to tell you before," Cy continued. "They know that now. They were afraid that it would spoil everything."

"You mean, our little game of happy families."

"No game, Thomas." Cy Gabriel looked serious. "Your happy family."

"Ex-family," I muttered.

"Tell me how you blew their cover."

I hesitated for a moment. It would be the first time I had spoken to someone not directly involved about the events which had changed my life. Instinctively, I wanted to hold on to my experience, keep it hidden, like my own private secret, but suddenly it occurred to me that there had been too many secrets in my shadowy little life. It was time for a bit of daylight.

"I've got this friend Gip," I said. "He's kind of a whiz with computers. He was here after school one day . . ."

It all came out—the file, Rendle, the coded adoption papers, even our weird visit to the Beast and his nutty mum. Cy was a good listener and talking to him was like losing this big sack of guilt that I had been lugging around with me all day.

"It was lucky you had someone to turn to," Cy said after I had finished speaking.

I sensed that Cy wanted me to tell him more but I was not about to blow the details of my friend's secret hide-away—not even to a stranger who would be flying back to America in a couple of days' time. "Yeah," I said. "He's all right is old Gip."

I heard my parents chatting upstairs. It seemed odd and

unlike them that they had left their guest unattended, particularly since the guest was meant to be their big boss-man.

"Sorry about the hosts," I said. "They seem to have gone walkabout."

"No problem. I arrived early." Cy paused as if something had just occurred to him. "You know what, Thomas? You need to get away from all this, take a break."

I was about to point out that I had only just returned from a holiday but he held up a hand. "Tomorrow I'm visiting our main depot over here. Limo, lunch, quick look around. Why not come along?"

Depot, limo, lunch? At any other time, the idea of spending the day at some lame workplace would have come a close second to a visit to the dentist as a way of spending my holiday time.

But to my surprise, I realized that the idea of a day away from home was what I wanted right now. It might even be interesting.

I heard the sound of voices as my ex-parents came down the stairs. If they became involved in any discussion about Cy's idea, I knew which way I would jump.

So I made a decision. "All right, then," I said.

"Deal," said Cy.

There was something unusual about this man. That night, over dinner, I began to get an idea of what it was. He had a simple, easy talent for making people feel good. At first, it bothered me. Who was this guy, this big-time American boss, who could just stroll into our lives and within seconds we were opening up like flowers in the sun? Was there some kind of trick involved, a creepy little technique they taught you at business school?

I fought against it and I lost. Cy was interested in other people. He seemed to want the best for them. His life had panned out pretty well and there was nothing he wanted more than to share his good fortune with the people he came into contact with. When strangers first met Gip, they would be suspicious of him. When they met the Beast, they would instinctively want to tease him. With Cy, they wanted to talk, to open up, to try to be as nice and easygoing as he was.

So, over dinner, I found myself joining in the conversation, sometimes even laughing, almost as if it was the old days and I was once more part of the family. At one point, late on in the meal, I caught my ex-mother's eye. She smiled at me and, before I could stop myself, I smiled back.

I was confused. It was as if the new me, Michael Garnham, was slipping away before I had even begun to understand him. Going to bed that night, I tried to feel within myself the burning anger that had become part of me over the past few days but somehow the friendliness and ease of that evening seemed to have doused the fire. I'm Michael, I whispered to myself, lying in bed but, as I drifted off to a dreamless sleep, I knew that Cy had been right. I was not Michael at all. I was Thomas Wisdom and there was no escaping from it.

Another thing. As hard as I tried to think of Mary and Mark Wisdom as fake family, former parents, I knew deep down that they were still my mum and my dad.

Late that night, when the house was dark and silent, I went downstairs and dialed Gip's number. "I need some help," I said.

"Shoot."

"I want to look for my real mother."

"All right, then. If you really want to."

"I do."

"Just don't pin your hopes, all right?"

"What d'you mean by that?"

"I know mothers," said Gip. "Doesn't do to put your trust in mothers."

Maybe it was because I just wanted to get out of the house but the next morning I woke early. Some time during the night Mum (she isn't my mum, and never has been, but I'm going to call her that from now on) had laid out some clothes for me on the chair near the bed but I took one glance at them and saw that they were the white-shirt-and-dark-trousers uniform that I'm forced into when weddings or Christmas come around. Sure, I wanted to please Cy Gabriel but there was a limit. I grabbed a T-shirt and jeans from my drawer. If the good folk of the Seraph Organization were shocked by that, it was their problem.

Cy rolled up in a flash, low-slung motor while my parents were still messing around upstairs getting ready for their day. It had worried me that we might all have to arrive at the office in one embarrassing gang but it turned out that the place Cy was taking me was some bigshot depot that Mr. and Mrs. Wisdom only visited once or twice a year themselves.

We drove. I'm never exactly talkative in the mornings and I was relieved that Cy was in relaxed, silent mode as well. He put on some classical music. The car whispered like a gray ghost through the town, and picked up speed when we hit a motorway. Surprisingly soon the scenery outside changed, rows of houses giving way to the golden stubble of summer cornfields. I watched the outside world as it raced by beyond the darkened windows and cool, air-conditioned comfort of the car.

At one point, I asked Cy where we were heading.

"West." He smiled at me. "The organization likes west."

"Right."

"You know why? Because west represents hope, the future. Man has always headed west. It's the next frontier. The east stands for lost hope, for erosion and age."

I looked at him to check whether he was taking the mickey out of me. He laughed again. "Go west, young man," he said.

I gazed out of the window, thinking all of a sudden of Gip and his hideaway out on the east of town. Then I pictured the neat suburban confidence of the west where we lived, which led as naturally as the course of a river into the opulent countryside I was looking at now.

Erosion. Hope. In a weird way, it all made sense.

We must have been driving for an hour or so when Cy swung off the motorway onto a small country road. We drove through one village, then another, before he stopped by an old-fashioned five-bar gate on the right of the road. Cy pressed something behind the lapel of his jacket and the gate swung open.

"The organization likes privacy," he said as we made our way down a narrow, high-banked road. After about a mile, we turned a bend. Without warning, the road opened out onto a big expanse of tarmac. A few hundred yards ahead of us, almost like a castle surrounded by a wide, solid moat, was a square white building.

Something of the look of it, the way it was designed, reminded me of the strange bunker I had visited that afternoon back in the desert beyond Seraph.

"Welcome to European HQ," he said, as we entered the car park where about fifty identical, executive-type motors were lined up as if for a race. Cy drew up in front of the building's main steps. He got out, stretched and, having taken his briefcase from the backseat, led me into the strangest office I had ever seen.

There was no receptionist. Doors opened before us as if somehow they could recognize that we belonged. We walked down a short corridor into a big, hall-like room. The bright screens of scores of computers gazed at us. In front of each of them was a man or a woman, gazing at the information in front of them as if their lives depended on it.

"This is where information comes through from all over the world." Cy spoke softly as if we were in a church or something. "Any tiny item of data that's relevant to our project is recorded, ordered, and deployed."

We walked between two of the rows of computers with their operators. Now and then he stopped by one of the workers, peered over a shoulder, at the screens, made a bit of small talk. When they became aware of his presence, each operative seemed to relax their concentration for a moment, more as if Cy was one of their best friends rather than the boss.

At the time I thought nothing odd of that, nor the fact that the information on the screens seemed to be in the form of numbers rather than words, but as we made our slow progress through the rooms I found it difficult to come up with the right kind of small talk.

"Wow," I said eventually. "All this for food."

"Yeah." The trace of a frown crossed Cy's face. "Food can be a complex business these days."

We took a lift to the first floor and he led me into his office, a big, bright room on the corner of the building with views over the rolling countryside.

"Want a drink?" Cy hung his jacket on the back of the door, wandered over to the corner and opened a fridge.

"Yeah. Yes, please," I said.

Cy took out two plastic bottles of sparkling water, handed one to me and opened his as he sat at his desk.

"Thomas, I've got a few calls to catch up on," he said casually. "Would you like to see a video about how this place works?"

A corporate video? Great, I thought gloomily. But I smiled and agreed.

For a moment, Cy stared at me as if considering whether to tell me something. Then he took a quick swig at the little bottle in his hand, stood up, and walked briskly to a small door on the far side of his office that I hadn't noticed before.

He opened it and, with a mock seriousness, ushered me in.

I stood on the threshold of the room. It was like a tiny cinema, with a couple of rows of comfortable seats in front of a large screen.

"I'm afraid we don't run to popcorn," said Cy as I sat down on one of the front-row seats. "Let me know if you need another drink."

I laid my bottle on the ledge of the chair.

"Enjoy." The voice of Cy was behind me but, when I turned to say something, he had closed the door behind him.

For a few seconds, I sat alone in the darkness. Then the screen flickered into life.

17 · PROJECT

HOW CAN I DESCRIBE WHAT happened next?

It was not like losing consciousness or being hypnotized or slipping into another reality. It was as if it was reality—more real than anything I had ever experienced but also more perfect and happy and peaceful. The everyday existence, which we all take for granted, suddenly seemed meaningless, full of futile argument and stress, like a restless dream.

The voices sounded, their music more beautiful than anything you have ever heard. A dark purple color, of a depth and warmth that no human painter or photographer has ever captured, filled the screen. I felt as if I was part of it, more serene and relaxed and content than I ever believed was possible. When the voice spoke, it was without sound—when I replied, it was by thought alone.

I was in the presence of the perfect parent, the perfect teacher, the perfect best friend. Together, we made the entire universe.

I was humble yet mighty, in control of all, yet as helpless as a new-born baby.

I had reached my destination.

YOU HAVE ARRIVED. IT HAS BEEN A LONG JOURNEY. YOU HAVE REQUIRED STRENGTH AND INTELLIGENCE TO REACH THIS PLACE. NOW YOU ARE HERE. THOMAS WISDOM, YOU ARE WELCOME.

Where am I?

YOU ARE BEYOND ALL LIMITS. NO HUMAN WORD EXISTS TO DESCRIBE THIS PLACE. IT IS FAR YET NEAR. BEYOND SPACE AND TIME YET WITHIN YOUR SOUL.

Am I on Earth?

YOU ARE CHOSEN. YOU ARE AMONG THE FEW, THE PRIVI-LEGED. IT IS YOU WHO WILL HELP US WITH OUR GREAT PROJ-ECT. ALL WILL BE DONE FOR THE GOOD OF THE EARTH, FOR THE SAVING OF HUMANKIND. THE PROJECT REQUIRES OF YOU ONLY TRUST.

What is the Project?

WE HAVE WATCHED YOUR WORLD. WE HAVE WATCHED AND WE HAVE DESPAIRED. YOU HAVE GROWN. YOU HAVE BEGUN TO UNDERSTAND THE PLANET WHERE YOU LIVE. YOU HAVE DEVELOPED THE MEANS TO BE STRONG AND TO SUR-VIVE. BUT WITH EVERY STEP FORWARD YOU MOVE NEARER THE ABYSS. WHAT YOU HAVE BEEN GIVEN FOR CREATION, YOU HAVE USED FOR DESTRUCTION. THE WISER YOU HAVE BECOME, THE MORE FOOLISHLY YOU HAVE BEHAVED. HUMAN-ITY IS STUMBLING AND FALLING. ITS LITTLE WORLD IS IN DANGER. IT NEEDS HELP.

AND YOU ARE HERE TO HELP US.

WE WATCHED FROM AFAR. WE DESPAIRED. THERE WERE THOSE WHO BELIEVED THAT EARTH SHOULD BE PERMITTED TO MEET ITS FATE. BUT WE ARE GOOD. WE BELIEVE YOU CAN

BE GOOD TOO. YOU NEED GUIDANCE TO BRING YOU OUT OF THE DARKNESS INTO THE LIGHT. WE HAVE SENT ANGELS TO SAVE YOU.

Angels?

ATTEND, THOMAS. ATTEND AND DO NOT FEAR. WE ARE GOOD. NOW THAT WE ARE HERE, YOU WILL BE SAFE. ANGELS ARE MOVING AMONG YOU. WE ARE GIVING YOU WHAT YOU LACKED, HEALING YOUR WOUNDS BEFORE YOU EVEN KNEW THAT YOU WERE SICK.

The Project.

THE PROJECT NEEDS YOU, YOU ARE AMONG THE CHOSEN. YOU SHALL BE GUIDED. YOU HAVE BEEN STRONG AND INTELLIGENT. NOW YOU ARE TO HELP US. ALL IS GOOD. ALL WILL BE RESOLVED.

ALL IS GOOD. ALL WILL BE RESOLVED.

YOU MUST TRUST US.

TRUST.

TRUST.

TRUST.

18 · ANGELS

I OPENED MY EYES and it took me several seconds to remember where I was. I had sunk down in the chair. The screen was blank in front of me. The air in the screening room seemed cool but, within me, there was a great warmth and sense of peace.

"Welcome back, Thomas."

The hand of Cy Gabriel was on my shoulder. Without thinking, I reached up and held on to it, eyes tightly shut. Then, gradually, I began to come round. I realized where I was, who I was. I released Cy's hand and looked at him.

He sat back in the seat beside me and smiled. A small leather-bound book was open in his lap.

"Did I sleep?" I asked.

"It wasn't exactly sleep."

"So it wasn't a dream."

Cy closed his book and sat forward in his seat. "It wasn't a dream, Thomas."

"What was it then?"

"You're going to have to forget everything you've ever assumed was true or logical." Cy spoke quietly. "You're about to believe the unbelievable."

Normally, I might have been frightened by what I was hearing but it was almost as if I had been slipped some kind of happiness pill. "Try me," I said quietly.

Cy Gabriel looked at the dark screen for a moment, then turned back to me. He seemed to tighten his grip on the book he was holding with both hands, almost as if it was the safety-bar on the roller-coaster that is edging forward at the start of a ride. When he spoke, it was in a quiet, deliberate voice.

"What you have just experienced is the Presence," he said. "The Presence is not a person or a thing or a voice. It is every person, every thing. Every voice you have heard comes from the Presence. It is in every thought. At the very center of your imagination, there is the Presence, day and night, from the moment you were born until the moment you die."

"Like God?" I asked warily. The happiness pill was beginning to wear off.

"No. Not like God at all. Nor like Buddha, Yahweh, Shiva, Allah. The Presence is beyond religion. It is not hope or faith. It is real."

There seemed no sensible reply to this. "Spooky," I said.

"Now, Thomas, I want you to imagine something." Cy hesitated and, for the first time, I realized that he was nervous. "Far away—further away than human mind can comprehend, there is a place like Earth, only different. It is occupied by a people that is similar to mankind but a mankind that has changed and developed. Time and space are no longer its masters, but its servants. It can live for as long as it wants. It has conquered the population problem.

It has discovered happiness. It can travel by thought. It can see beyond what you now understand as the universe into other universes, billions and billions of miles away. And one day—" Cy closed his eyes. "One day, this planet discovers it is not alone. There is life elsewhere, developing in its own strange, slow way. Its people—the people you are imagining—watch from afar."

"But how could they do that if—?"

"They watch, Thomas." For the first time, there was a hint of impatience in Cy's voice. "So we go forward another thousand years, more. And, guess what, the life on that distant planet is developing, but not in the way humankind had hoped. It fights. It kills. Its greed is ever-growing and seems as if it will never be satisfied. What should be done about this? Should the poor, distant, little planet be left to its fate? Should the watchers do nothing to help?"

I frowned, hearing an echo in Cy's words of what the voice behind the screen had been saying to me. "Not if it's good," I said softly.

"Not if it's good." His eyes were unblinking as they stared at me. I had been given the clues. It was for me to make the jump into the unknown.

"The poor, distant, little planet is us, isn't it? This . . . Presence thing has been watching us from out there in the universe."

"Beyond what you think of as the universe."

A chill of fear ran through me. "And now it's here."

"Yes." Cy smiled and I knew that I'd passed some sort of test. "Now we're here."

He took me back to his office where he gave me a glass of water. The midday sun shone through the darkened windows and, sipping slowly at the drink in my hand, I gazed at the field, the hedges, the trees, as if I were seeing them for the first time.

Gently, Cy guided me to the chair in front of his desk. I sat down. He slumped into his own chair and rubbed his eyes.

"There is a planet so far away from here that no human astronomer would ever dream of its existence," he said. "It has no name but it has its own highly advanced form of life. At first, when it discovered the existence of life on Earth, it was pleased. One day, when humanity was ready, it would visit. The two life forces in the universe would unite in friendship. It waited for hundreds of years. But something went wrong, not there but on Earth. Humankind seemed to take a wrong turning in its development. Those on that distant planet realized the life on Earth was so programmed to destructiveness that any contact was out of the question. Humankind would do what it always did when it was afraid. It would make war. Because it was so undeveloped, this would be like a two-year-old child attacking a tiger. It would be destroyed. So they left Earth alone."

Cy gazed out of the window for a moment, then started talking again. "But Earth did not leave itself alone. It used knowledge against itself. It developed the means to destroy itself. The distant power, the planet of the Presence, could not watch and do nothing as another life form snuffed itself out. So it developed the Project. It would join humankind. It would save Earth from within. It would send its own beings to guide humankind away from the path of death and destruction towards good. It would make angels on the surface of the Earth. The angels would work with humankind in a project of salvation."

"You're an angel," I whispered.

Cy nodded slowly.

"And my parents. They come from this distant planet too?"

"They were created here. But they're angels."

I thought of my mother and father for a moment. I saw Mum collecting me from school, Dad watching me as I played football in the park.

"But they're so normal," I said. "So ordinary."

"Angels are normal. They are essentially humans but . . . without the bad bits."

Cy Gabriel gazed at me across the desk, gently smiling. I became aware that my mouth was dry, my hands were clasped around the empty glass in my hand.

"I think I'd like to wake up now, please," I said faintly.

Leaning forward, Cy turned the monitor on his desk towards me. The screen, which had been full of numbers became a pixelated haze. When it cleared, I was staring at the face of a young, blonde woman.

"She's one of our people downstairs," said Cy. "As she works on the screen, I can watch her—or anyone else down there."

"Kind of like spying." My voice sounded more hostile than I had intended.

Cy smiled patiently. "We tend not to think like that," he said. "Her name's Hazel. She's working here for a while. She'll be leaving us within a few weeks."

"Yeah?"

"She's an angel."

"Yeah, she's not bad, I supp—" I blushed, realizing my mistake. "Oh, you mean, she's not from here."

"How old would you say she was, Thomas?"

"Twenty-five? Maybe thirty."

"She was born—she was made—two weeks ago."

I think I swore at that point. It seemed like the only logical reaction. "You don't expect me to believe all this," I said weakly.

He leaned forward and touched the screen. The blonde

woman's eyes refocused and she smiled. "Hi, Cy," she said as normal as you'd like.

"Hi, Hazel. Would you mind coming up for a moment? There's someone I'd like you to meet."

"Sure."

As the woman left her desk, the screen turned to the lists of numbers that had been there before.

I must have been looking kind of out of it because Cy said, "I realize this is a lot to take in, Thomas, but you'll get tuned in soon. Right now you're thinking that the Project is unnatural but it's not. It's just a different kind of nature."

Why me? That was the question which was suddenly the one I wanted to ask, which filled my entire being. Why? Me?

There was a knock on the office door and, without waiting for a reply, the blonde woman—the angel—who had been on Cy's screen a moment ago, entered the room.

"Hazel, this is Thomas Wisdom, a good friend of mine. Thomas, my colleague Hazel Webb."

The woman stepped forward. "Hi, Thomas," she said. Her hand when she shook mine was cool and smooth, but it was not the hand of a robot.

"Hi."

"Thomas knows about the Project," said Cy.

"Ah." Hazel Webb raised her eyebrows in that quick, clever way girls have of expressing mild surprise.

Hazel sat down and crossed her legs. "I'm twenty-six," she said. "I've been here a short time and have recently been accepted for a post in a head-hunting employment agency, which I shall be taking up next month." She smiled like someone at a job interview. Although she was neat and could talk easily and without hesitation, there was, to be honest, nothing weird about her. She was what they call the "girl next door" type.

Cy crossed his arms and frowned jokily. "And what about the personal stuff?"

To my surprise, Hazel seemed embarrassed. "I'm going out with a certain person," she said, her eyes on Cy. "We're engaged and hope to be married next year."

A thought occurred to me. "Is he—? I mean, where did you meet him?"

Hazel glanced at me and I sensed that I had gone too far. Angels had feelings too, it turned out.

"He's a colleague," she said coolly.

For a moment there was silence in the office. Then Cy leaned forward and said, in a mock confidential voice. "Why don't you show him your derm, Hazel?"

Derm? Derm? It seemed rude to ask what exactly he was talking about.

"You really want to see my derm?" Hazel asked, turning in her chair.

Now it was my turn to blush.

"Not . . . necessarily," I said.

She pulled her blouse back slightly. On her collar-bone was a dark, red patch of skin, like a small birthmark.

I looked at it politely and said, "Oh yeah" as if I really understood what this was all about.

"That little mark is more important to Hazel than her heart," said Cy. "It's a circuit that provides her with all the information and energy she needs from day to day. We all have one." He drew back the left sleeve of his jacket. There, showing through the silver hairs on his tanned forearm, was the red, circular mark I had noticed at dinner in Santa Barbara. It was identical to Hazel's.

"Give me your hand," he said, stretching his arm out to me.

Nervously, I reached out my hand. Like a policeman

taking a fingerprint, he took the index finger and placed it firmly on his arm.

"Sheesh!" I jumped back, startled. The flesh all around the derm was normal and warm but the spot itself radiated ice-cold.

They both laughed.

Cy smiled, first at Hazel, then at me. "We are built like human beings—except in that one tiny area."

"You've got that re-charging thing," I said. "You're like a mobile phone disguised as a human."

Cy held up two hands, less amused now. "Hey, easy," he said. "I didn't bring you here to get insulted."

I was about to tell him that I wanted to go home. Then I realized that home was no longer home. My mind was filled with a million questions but right now one mattered more than all the rest put together.

"So, why did you tell me all this?" I asked.

Cy gazed at me across the desk, and sighed.

"Go on then," I said. "Why me? Why am I here?"

He turned to Hazel with a boss-like smile. "Thanks, Hazel," he said. "Could you excuse us?"

The blonde angel stood up. "Good luck, Thomas," she said. Then she left, closing the door behind her.

"You want me to show you around the place before we grab some lunch?" Cy asked.

"Sure," I said. "When you've answered my question."

"You're tougher than you look, Thomas Wisdom," he said with a smile that somehow didn't convey much humor.

I sat back in my chair and folded my arms.

"Why me?"

The smile seemed to freeze on his face. He gazed at me unblinkingly for a moment or two.

"I'd like you to talk to your mom and dad about that.

Right now, let's just say that angels can't complete the Project alone. We need help from the next generation."

"Does Amy know about this?" I asked eventually.

"Sure."

"When did you tell her?"

Cy hesitated. "She didn't need to be told."

It took a second or two for me to understand what he was telling me. "You mean . . . she's an angel too?"

"Yup. And Luke."

I shook my head. "I don't believe this," I muttered. "I'm the only person in our house who was actually born on Earth in the normal way. Me and Dougal."

Cy winced and shook his head.

Now I'd heard it all. "You're not telling me that Dougal's an angel?"

"He's one of our better models."

"I always wondered why he was a bit crazy."

Cy remained straight-faced.

"Angels aren't crazy, Thomas," he said. "We are just minor variations on the standard human and animal model who happen to have arrived here by a different route."

"I should say." Somehow the idea of angel animals was more difficult to take on board than anything else. "So all over the world there are these pets who have been manufactured by aliens—angel dogs, angel cats, angel hamsters, angel gerbils."

Cy frowned. "Not cats, as it happens," he murmured. "Dogs were a piece of cake to replicate but we couldn't do the cat thing. We're still working on that."

"Which is why cats always run away from my parents."

"Guess so." Cy seemed slightly irritated by the direction the conversation had taken. He glanced at his watch and stood up. "Let's go get some lunch," he said. "Then I'll show you around."

I followed him out of the office. We took the lift down to the first floor where we walked again past the rows of computers.

I looked more closely at their operators now. Most of them seemed to be in their twenties or thirties. The majority had light hair. Apart from that, there was nothing spooky or unusual about them. They worked. They answered telephones. They chatted. Some of them glanced up as we walked past.

Cy pushed through some swing doors ahead of me. We were in a light, high-ceilinged room. To our right, food was being served to a queue of angels with trays.

"Canteen," I said stupidly.

"Canteen." Cy handed me a tray. "Food. Drink. Lunch."

"I can't get used to how normal everything is."

As we queued, Cy lowered his voice. "You've got to shake off these prejudices of yours, Thomas," he said. "We don't just look the same as you. We feel the same as you. Heat, cold, fear, anger—" He hesitated. "Love."

I thought of my family of angels with their cute little angel dog.

As if he could read my mind, Cy said, "Mark and Mary love you like any parents would do—maybe more. It's not every son who gets to help with the Project."

A woman in a white coat was serving up shepherd's pie. She smiled at me confidentially as she served me as if she, like everyone else, knew why I was here. I realized that I had been so startled by the news Cy had given me about my family that I had forgotten to press him on where exactly I fitted into this famous Project of theirs.

"What help?" I asked when we had taken a table by the window. "What do you need me for?"

Cy shrugged. "Nothing too difficult," he said. "When you leave school, we'd like you to work in a certain area we'll tell you about later. You'll be a success at it—we'll make sure about that. Then you'll just go on and live your life in the way you see fit."

"Except I have to do the job you tell me to."

"We can discuss your career when the moment comes," Cy said smoothly. "I don't anticipate that we'll disagree."

"I dunno." I shook my head. "I was always kind of keen on the idea of making up my own mind about my life."

"You will. We'll just be there to offer advice."

"Angels to watch over me." As I said these words, half-joking, I experienced an odd sense of pride that I had been selected to play my part in the Project.

"We understand your concern about personal freedom. You probably hadn't figured on saving the world as a career option."

"Not exactly."

Cy smiled. "That's what we like about you. The world-savers are usually the dangerous ones."

So we chatted on. If you had caught sight of us through that big plate-glass window, you might have mistaken me for a guy telling his uncle what he had done on his holidays. In fact, we were talking about the Project, the Presence, and how angels were going to save humanity from itself.

But the events of that morning were beginning to have an effect on me. As soon as I finished my meal, I felt weary to my bones.

We stopped talking. Cy led me back to his car. Within minutes of his reaching the motorway, my head had slumped against the window and I was fast asleep.

19 · REBORN

NOW, WHEN I READ BACK over what I have written, I am amazed. A man, a virtual stranger, had taken me to an office. He had put me in front of a screen where I had had a sort of dream-conversation with a God-like voice in my head. The stranger had told me that my parents, my sister, and even my damn family dog were in fact from another planet. Oh yeah, and I had been chosen to help them all save the world from destruction.

I had believed it all because I knew that it was true.

Yet, rather than feeling terror and panic, a sort of mellowness crept over me. I was chosen. Everything in my life had an explanation. There was a plan and I was part of it. The mess and anger and confusion of the past were gone. I felt reborn.

Home was home once more. When Cy Gabriel brought me back that afternoon, I walked sleepily up the garden path. The door opened ahead of me. As if they had been waiting for me all day, Mum and Dad stood in the hall, with Amy just behind them and Dougal, wagging his stump of a tail, at her ankles. Mum opened her arms and I leaned against her for a few seconds, feeling her warmth against me.

"Well done, darling," she whispered through my hair.

I was no longer the outsider in the family. I belonged. I was loved.

Behind me, Cy said something about the day having gone perfectly. He had a meeting in town, he said. He laid a hand on my shoulder, squeezed slightly and told me he'd see me again soon. Still in my mother's arms, I thanked him and said goodbye. The front door closed.

We went to the sitting-room. On the table in front of the sofa, there was a silver bucket containing a bottle of champagne in it and four glasses. Dad unwrapped the gold foil, popped the cork, poured frothing champagne into each glass. Still standing, we raised our glasses. For a moment, I thought we would be toasting the Project or there would be some sort of extraterrestrial greeting but they all smiled and said after one another, all loving and solemn.

"To Thomas."

"To Thomas."

"To Thomas."

"Yeah, right," I said, embarrassed but pleased. "To me."

So it went on. The family together, the family repaired. For that evening and all the next day, Mum, Dad, Amy, and me talked and laughed about the adventure that was our lives.

They told me about being an angel.

"D'you feel different?" I asked, later that evening.

"Not at all," said my mother. "The danger is that you forget that you're not quite like other humans."

"Dare I ask in what way?"

"Configurations," said Amy, rolling her eyes, and all three of them laughed as if at some great private joke.

"What exactly are configurations?" I asked.

"We each have a derm." My father touched his shoulder, as if to reassure himself that his derm was still in place. "If possible, the information in the derm needs to be configured once a day. All we need is the presence of water and what we call a derm-node that receives messages from a transmitter. It's like a little metal plaque."

I remembered Gip's discovery on the wall of the house all those weeks ago. "The loo," I said. "You configure in the loo."

My mum smiled. "It only takes a few seconds."

"You know that new style of public toilet that has been appearing over the last few years?" My sister seemed particularly amused by this subject. "They were made for angels. Now we can configure anywhere we want."

"But what I don't get is why you don't just save the Earth yourselves? Why do you need the help of human beings? Where do I fit into all this?"

For the first time, I sensed awkwardness in my little family. After a few moments, Dad said, "It is important that humankind is involved in its own salvation."

"Otherwise, it could happen all over again," said my mother.

"Yeah?" There was more. I knew there was more. I could see it in their eyes.

It was Amy who cracked. "Mum? Dad?" she said. "That's not exactly the whole story, is it?"

My parents concentrated on eating their food. "Let's change the subject," Dad said eventually.

"So I'm part of the team except I'm not meant to know

what's really going on," I said. "That's just great."

"It's embarrassing," said my mother quietly. "It's not the sort of thing one should talk about."

I was beginning to get an uncomfortable idea of what the problem was when Amy turned to me with a sisterly smile. "Angels can't reproduce," she said.

"Ah."

My parents stared at the floor. "In every sense, we are human," Dad said eventually. "We feel emotion, we love, we hate, we laugh, we are vulnerable. But we don't . . . have babies. That is the one human function which is beyond our power."

"So you adopt," I whispered.

My mother covered my hand with hers and squeezed it tightly. "We adopt," she said.

I was not upset. I was calm. Through all this—this conversation and many more—I was aware of a serene sense of peace within me which I had never experienced before.

Nothing could hurt me. I was part of the Project.

Twice, as I talked to my family, the telephone rang, once in the morning and once in the evening. It was Gip Sanchez. He seemed kind of anxious about me.

A chill entered my heart. I no longer wished to speak to him. It was almost as if, overnight, he had become my enemy. I answered his questions briefly and coldly. I told him I would see him some time. No, he shouldn't call me. I would call him.

Why did I feel like this? Why was I so happy and warm within my family of angels? What had Gip done to set himself outside the walls I had built around myself?

I understood none of that then.

I do now.

There are some people who find it difficult to take a

hint. It's not that they don't want to be helpful or fit in with other people so much as a sort of deafness. It's as if they have been born without the gene that helps one human being understand another. The world hints and prods and nudges at them but they hear and feel nothing.

Rendle was like that—he never understood what was really going on in class until it was too late—and so was Luke the Surfer-Boy, although that might have been just good old-fashioned thickness. But nobody—that is, nobody—was better at hint-deafness than Gip Sanchez.

People laughed at him, bullied him, made jokes about his spots or his hair or his leg or his mum. A few even pitied him. It was all the same to Gip. It was not that he ignored them—he had never really seen them in the first place. Somewhere along the line, maybe early in his strange, rackety life, he had built this protective shell around him.

Now, for the first time in our friendship, I wished that just occasionally Gip could take a hint.

On my first morning alone since discovering the truth about my family, he telephoned in the middle of the morning.

"Yo," he said. "How you been?"

"Hello, Gip."

"We've really got to meet today. There are things going down, Colin-wise."

"Yeah?" I put as much lack of interest into the one word as I could manage. The truth was, ever since my day with Cy, I had been feeling woozy and tired, as if I was recovering from flu or something. "You know, Gip, I'm not feeling too clever right now. I fancy a day vegging out."

"Fine. I'll swing by in about half an hour then."

"Um, no."

"OK. So meet me at the flat."

I gave it a couple of seconds' thought before deciding that, right then, seeing Gip in his unofficial hangout would be preferable to him paying a visit to me in my house. Grumpily, I agreed to meet him at the squat in a couple of hours.

So I traveled across town—bus, train, walk. As I watched the townscape, it was as if I was seeing the world as it really was for the first time. The dead-eyed people on the bus, the mobile-phone twitchies, talking as they walked as if their lives depended on it, the traffic, the grimy pavements, the underground users descending into burrows beneath the city like zombie rabbits, the dossers slumped on pavements and platforms, hands out for money, their watching eyes expressing a flicker of hope before returning to despair as we pass. Spare change, mate? Spare change? Got any spare change, please?

And I knew that Cy was right. Humankind had lost the plot. The Project was good. They needed the help of the Presence. We needed it. I needed it.

When I reached the squat, Gip greeted me at the door.

"So?" he said as we climbed the stairs. "How was your day with good old Cy?"

"Fine," I muttered.

Gip glanced back at me.

"Interesting," I added.

"And?"

"That food development business is . . . kind of cool."

He waited until we reached the room on the top floor before speaking again and when he did it was with unusual seriousness. "Don't give me all this," he said suddenly. "Three days ago, we were together on this whole family, adoption thing. Now you're coming on like nothing happened. You even look different."

I heard the words in my head— "I am different"—but something stopped me from speaking them. "I'm kind of zonked."

To my surprise, Gip put a hand to my forehead, just like a mum. "Bull," he said briskly. "There's something going on and you're holding back on me."

"It's my life. For you, it may be just an adventure but this is my life, my family, my home." I wandered over to the window and was sitting on the floor, looking at the motorway when something occurred to me. "How did you know where I was?" I asked.

"Mmm?" Gip acted casual but I wasn't taken in.

"I never told you I was with Cy Gabriel but you asked me how my day with him went."

"Oh that. I was kind of worried about you so I called to see how you were. Your mum told me about your little outing."

For a moment, we stared at one another. Somehow the idea of Gip Sanchez as Mr. Concerned didn't quite cut it for me. "You mentioned Rendle," I said coldly.

"He started calling me. He seemed worried about you."

"Yeah yeah. The Beast with the heart."

"He's told the Head."

I stared at him for a moment. "You're kidding."

Gip shook his head. "He said that he had become more and more concerned. Because of him, you had got hold of this bit of life-shattering news about your life. He had decided he couldn't just leave it there. So he rang Daisy."

Daisy Dover, the head teacher, was a big favorite among the parents and the local councilors—they said that he had "turned the school around," whatever that meant—but, to me, he seemed to have as much warmth and sympathy as a dead fish on a slab. I hated the idea of him taking possession of my big news and adding it to the little folder under my name in his office.

"That's why I needed to see you." Gip spoke quietly. "I told him he could have talked to me but he started giving me this load of old rubbish about teachers' responsibilities—how, if anything should happen, it could destroy his career."

"Big tragedy that would be," I murmured. Although I understood that none of it was entirely Gip's fault, I didn't like the idea of him chatting away to the Beast about me and my life. I had thought we were in this together. "So what did Dover say?"

"He thanked Colin and said he would have to consider what to do."

"He'll call my parents."

"Maybe. He might just have a cozy chat with you next term."

I laughed briefly. Daisy Dover, a pale, neat man in his late thirties, was not exactly famous for his charm and sympathetic manner.

Gip wasn't smiling. "I've called Colin a few times since then. There's no answer."

"Maybe he went on holiday."

Gip shook his head and his long hair swayed like a dark curtain disturbed by the wind. "Colin doesn't do holidays."

"His mother probably got sick," I said, thinking more about how he betrayed me than any little problem he might now be having. "I wouldn't sweat about it, if I were you."

"I'm not sweating," said Gip quietly. "But I'm calling him tonight. If there's no reply, I'm going round there tomorrow."

"Suit yourself."

Gip gave me that long, wordless stare that I knew so well. I held out for about five seconds.

"All right. I'll come along with you."

"Thanks, Tom. You're all heart."

There was a chill between us that was new. It made me sad but there was nothing I could do about it.

I was in for another surprise that night. When I got home, Mum and Dad greeted me at the door and led me upstairs to my room. On my bed was a large cardboard box. I opened the top and saw what was inside.

"A computer! I don't believe this." I looked at the manual. Although I'm not exactly an expert on computers, I knew my parents well enough to know that it would be a good one.

I turned back to them. "But why?"

"You've had a tough time recently, old boy," said my father. "It was a thank-you from us."

I walked over and hugged my mother. Dad put his hand on my shoulder. We stood there for a moment, saying nothing, just holding on to each other.

"Thanks, Dad. Thanks, Mum," I said at last.

And I knew that those words, "Mum, Dad," were what they wanted to hear above all else.

20 · ACCIDENT

WHEN GIP TURNED UP on my doorstep the next morning, I told him about the computer. He has always been something of a techno-freak and I expected him at least to want to know stuff about its memory, make, and capacity.

But he gave me an odd look. "Yeah, the old computer," he said almost shiftily. "That figures."

I asked him what he meant, told him that my parents didn't need to buy themselves back into my favor, but he turned away and started walking down the garden path. "We'll talk about that later," he called back over his shoulder. "You coming?"

That was the way it was with Gip. Most of the time, he's Mr. Cruise Control, taking everything in his stride, but then, suddenly and without warning, he changes. The eyes narrow, the smile goes, and so do the words. He becomes cold and determined and focused on the target of the moment.

I walked beside him in silence.

We sat on the bus like an old married couple who had just had a row. We took the road to the Beast's house as grimly as gunslingers at high noon. By the time he rang the front doorbell, I had more or less decided that maybe Gip Sanchez was not my friend anymore.

A stranger opened the door—a plump, middle-aged woman with gray-blonde hair. She was wearing the blue uniform of a nurse.

"Is Mr. Rendle in, please?" Gip asked.

"Mr. Rendle?" The woman seemed strangely startled. "No, he's . . . he's not here."

"When will he be back?"

An uneasy look—part concerned, part irritated—crossed the woman's face. "Are you friends of his?" she asked.

"We go to his school," said Gip. "He teaches us math."

The woman extended her hand. "I'm Joan," she said. "I've been looking after Mrs. Rendle."

Something was going on here. As if she had suddenly reached a decision, the woman called Joan stepped back into the hall. "Come in, boys," she said.

Closing the door behind us, she turned and said, "There's been a bit of an accident."

"What kind of accident?" Gip's question was abrupt, almost rude.

"A motor accident," said Joan. "I'm afraid I have very sad news, boys. Colin Rendle has, very tragically, been involved in a fatal crash."

Gip shook his head. "But he doesn't drive."

That word "fatal" told me all I needed to know. "He's dead, isn't he?"

The woman lowered her head and nodded slowly. "He

stepped off a pavement while out for a walk last Monday. A car came out of nowhere." She spoke quietly, almost in a whisper. "He was gone by the time the ambulance arrived."

Gip and I stood there stupidly in silence for several seconds. "I don't believe it," I murmured. "He can't be dead."

"I'm very, very sorry." Joan spoke gently. "I never met the gentleman personally but I believe he was a very special man. I was called in by the council because our records showed there was a Mrs. Rendle."

Briefly, I thought that another shock was on the way, that suddenly a Mrs. Beast was about to be revealed. Then I remembered the old lady who was Rendle's mother. "How's she taking it?" I asked.

"She's confused, poor love."

"Maybe we should just say hello." I glanced across at Gip.

He said nothing but stared into Joan's face, his dark eyes sparkling against his deathly pale complexion. He seemed to be having trouble breathing.

"Gip?" I said.

Slowly he turned towards me. "They killed him." He shook his head. "How could they do that? They killed him. He had done nothing."

I laid a hand on his shoulder but he shrugged it off.

Joan seemed uneasy at the way Gip was reacting. "I'm sorry, I shouldn't have told you," she said. "I had no idea you were so . . . close. Maybe you should go home to your—"

"We'll see Mrs. Rendle," Gip interrupted, his voice hard now. He walked past her towards the sitting-room.

"She's under sedation." The nurse followed him. "She's not quite aware of what's happened."

When I entered the sitting-room, Gip was crouched in

front of the old woman. The room was darker than when we had last been here and Mrs. Rendle seemed to have shrunk over the past few days. She was just a gray wisp of a thing.

"All right, Mrs. Rendle?" Gip laid a hand on hers. "We just called by to see how you were doing."

"Hello, boys." The old woman's voice sounded like rustling leaves. "Have you been with that naughty Colin?"

"Er, no, we haven't," said Gip.

"I don't know." She shook her head slightly and clicked her teeth. "He said he had to see the headmaster but he's been ages now. Always late, that boy."

There seemed nothing that we could say.

"Matron's been looking for him." Slowly and with great effort, she looked up at Joan. "Haven't you, Matron?"

"I have, Mrs. Rendle." Joan smiled sadly.

Mrs. Rendle closed her eyes and, for a moment, I thought she had gone to sleep. But when she opened them, she was looking at me. "Are you in the same class as Colin?"

"Er, no," I said quickly. "We're in a different year."

"He's quite bright, you know." She sighed wearily. "More brains than sense, though. He was frightened of that headmaster."

I noticed that Gip was trembling now. It occurred to me that he might say something that would upset the old woman.

"We'd better not stay too long," I muttered.

"Thanks for calling by, boys." Mrs. Rendle spoke almost cheerfully. "If you see Colin, tell him to hurry back." She shook her head sadly. "You know, he didn't even take his lunch with him. I made him sandwiches. Ham, it was, his favorite. Or was it egg?"

Joan stepped forward. She leaned over Mrs. Rendle, and

pulled the blanket up around the old woman's tiny wrinkled neck. For just the briefest moment, I saw something that made me draw in my breath in a sudden gasp.

Gip stood up slowly and walked past me to the door.

"Thank you for your visit, boys." Joan spoke, her back to us. "Could you let yourselves out?"

We nodded and said goodbye to Mrs. Rendle.

"He's such a naughty boy," she said, more to herself than to us.

We left, walking slowly down the street. After a few yards, we came to a low wall. Without a word, Gip dropped on to it and buried his face in his hands. He rocked backwards and forwards, making a low, rhythmic moan like some sort of animal in pain. I sat beside him, not knowing quite what to say. After a few seconds, I realized that the sound he was making were words, repeated again and again.

"It was me, it was me, it was me, it was me . . ."

"Come on, Gip," I said. "You know how absent-minded he was. It wasn't anything to do with the business of the file—it was an accident."

He looked up sharply, his eyes burning into mine with what almost seemed like hatred. "You know nothing," he said. "Nothing about anything."

I retreated into myself. Turning my back on him, I gazed at the house where Rendle had once lived.

I did know something and it filled my heart with dread and confusion.

Before me, in my mind's eye, I saw the figure of the nurse, Joan, as she crouched over Mrs. Rendle. She had extended an arm, lifting the blanket. At that moment, it was as clear as daylight. There could be no mistaking it. Where her neck joined her shoulder was a dark, circular mark.

It might have been a mole. It could have been a

birthmark. But I knew, with a cold, frightening certainty, that it was neither.

It was a derm.

We walked. We passed the bus stop. We reached the main road, not saying a word to one another.

Right now, silence suited me just fine. The nurse looking after Mrs. Rendle was an angel. I tried, again and again, to find an innocent, logical reason for it.

Angels were everywhere. What could be more natural than for one to be helping an old lady in her hour of need? Angels were here to help humanity. Joan seemed a kind, normal person. There was no need to be afraid. Angels were good. The idea that Rendle might be a victim of them was crazy. Why should they be worried about some math teacher? It was impossible. No, angels were good.

We walked until we reached my front gate. Gip stood there, hands in pockets, staring at the pavement, like someone being scolded by a voice in his head.

"Tomorrow?" I said.

"Yeah." Gip nodded, turned and limped off down the road.

My parents were back early from work. Hearing their voices in low discussion in the sitting-room, I went upstairs to my room and sat in front of the computer for a while, playing a game.

Mysteriously, it calmed me down. The terrible possibility that what Cy Gabriel had called the Project might involve killing and harming people was smoothed away by the sharp rhythms of the game. After a minute or two, I relaxed. Accidents happened. I could see that now. Gip would see it too in a couple of days' time. There was no need even to tell him about the Project or the Presence or Cy or my parents. Everything was good. Everything was going to be all right.

After some time, as I played, I felt the hand of my mother on my shoulder. She kissed the crown of my head.

"How's the computer?" she asked softly.

"It's good," I said.

"The games on it are OK?"

"They're fine." I zapped a guy with a machine-gun who was guarding the entrance to a cave. "Die, sucker," I muttered.

My mother sighed. "They're so violent, these games," she said.

"The bad guys get it, don't they?" I said, taking out a parachute descending on the right-hand side of the screen. "That's just the way it is."

I felt the hand on my shoulder tighten slightly and I sensed that she was about to say something, but then thought better of it. "Supper's in ten minutes," she said.

I played on, my mind calm and easy like that of a champion poker player.

21 · EVIL

THAT NIGHT I SLEPT HEAVILY but it was not a dreamless sleep. I awoke the next morning, knowing that during the night a message of profound importance had reached me. It was a warning, simple and impossible to ignore.

SANCHEZ IS EVIL. HE SEEMS GOOD BUT HE WILL DO YOU HARM. YOU MUST EXCLUDE HIM FROM YOUR LIFE.

I lay in bed. My limbs were heavy, my mind sluggish and numb. At some point, I was aware that the front doorbell was ringing. Dougal barked downstairs. I got up from my bed and stood on the landing. I saw a shape through the glass of the front door, heard someone call my name. It was Gip.

That day, I needed to be alone. I went back to bed.

It was one of those days when even thinking seems too much like hard work. I lay on the bed. I dozed. I played the computer. Later that morning, Dougal scratched at the door. When I let him in, he whined and looked up at me as if to remind me that even angel-dogs have needs.

I slobbed into some clothes and out of the house, following Dougal in the direction of the park. Somewhere at the back of my mind was the niggling memory of yesterday's events—of hearing about Rendle's death, of the nurse and her derm—but, for reasons I was unable to understand, none of that seemed to touch my life anymore.

I was a boy walking his dog in the park. All would be good. All would be resolved.

I stood under a cherry tree and watched Dougal. Like me, he has his lazy days but right now he ranged about the place on his own little adventure, pretending to himself that he was a wild beast, a stranger to domestic life.

Then, beyond him, I saw a familiar figure enter the park through its big iron gate and limp determinedly towards me. Dougal was too far away for me to be able to escape.

"I've got news," Gip called out as he approached me. "We need to talk."

I looked away. "I'm not in the mood," I murmured.

Gip looked into my eyes. "You've been on that computer, haven't you?"

"How did you know that?"

"No big deal, it's what computers do to you." He spoke hurriedly, like someone who had more important things to discuss. "Rendle's death wasn't an accident," he said. "He was taken out by the Firm because he knew too much."

"This isn't a movie, Gip," I said wearily. "A klutzy teacher with stuff on his mind stepped into the road in front of a speeding car. It happens."

Gip reached into his back pocket and took out some papers. He passed me the top sheet. "Take a look at who was driving that speeding car."

It was a photocopy from a local paper. *Teacher Dies In Police Car Tragedy*, read the headline. "The cops," said Gip with a grim little smile. "He was killed by the cops."

I scanned the news-story quickly. Rendle had been hit while crossing the main road on his way to the shops one afternoon. A police car, answering an emergency call, had turned the corner at high speed and had no chance of avoiding him. There was to be "a full police enquiry".

I handed the photocopy back. "Those guys drive too fast," I said. "You read about this kind of thing all the time."

"With no siren? Down a busy street?"

I shrugged. "So why would the CIA want to murder a math teacher?" I asked.

Gip handed me the other two sheets of paper. "I checked him on the Net," he said. "It turns out that Colin was a bit more than your average teacher."

I looked at the photocopies. The first sheet, which seemed to be some kind of nerdy student essay, was headed Digital Modifications to the Rendle Circuit Inducer. For all I could understand, every word might have been in a foreign language.

"Now check out the other one," said Gip.

This was a shorter report, which seemed to have been taken from some kind of on-line science magazine.

Avionics community mourns
"black box" pioneer
Dr. Colin Rendle, whose work on circuit induction played a crucial part in the development of the modern "black box" flight recorder, has been killed in a motor accident in London. During his seven years at Marconi Instruments during the 1980s, Rendle pioneered the titration caliber system, a version of which is used in many passenger aircraft to this day. Rendle retired from

scientific research in 1991 following a spell of ill-health.
At the time of his death, he was a teacher of mathemat-
ics in a London Secondary School.

"So the rumors were true." I passed the photocopies
back to Gip. "Old Rendle was a famous scientist."

"Maybe he knew something," said Gip. "He got out of
research because he discovered that his work was being
used for weapon guidance systems, OK? They've been
tracking him ever since." Gip glanced towards the gate, as if
expecting to see a squad of CIA hitmen, their jackets
bulging with weaponry, entering the park.

"You've lost it," I said. "You've gone paranoiac on me
again." I passed him back the papers.

Exhausted by his burst of exercise, Dougal had returned
and sat at my feet with an expression suggesting that he had
had enough of the wild prairies of the park and wanted to
go home. "I've got to get back," I said and started walking
away.

"Another thing," Gip called after me. "I put in a call to
Daisy Dover."

I stopped. "What's it got to do with him?"

"Colin might have told him something. The Head was
probably one of the last people he spoke to."

"So what did old Daisy have to say?"

Gip walked up to me slowly. "Tragic accident, talented
teacher cut down in his prime, blah blah blah. I told him I
knew that Colin had rung him about your adoption thing."

"My adoption thing. Thanks, Gip."

"He seemed to know all about it. He asked how you were
taking it. I said you were kind of freaked. We chatted. Then
he said, 'Goodbye, Gary,' and hung up."

"I told you he wouldn't help you."

"But he did." Gip smiled. "While we were talking about your adoption, he happened to tell me where your real mother comes from."

I stared at him for moment, not believing what I had just heard.

"It's a place called Cromer, in Norfolk," he said. "Fancy a little trip?"

I called Dougal but he refused to follow. Wearily, I turned and picked him up.

Gip shook his head. "Your dog, man. It's a total nutter."

I gave an angry little laugh. "That's good coming from you." With as much dignity as someone carrying a fat little dog in his arms can manage, I walked away.

"I could get us a lift up there," Gip called after me.

I made my way back home, wondering why, suddenly, I was so wary of Gip and his plans. Part of me, the old Thomas Wisdom, wanted to run down the street, to tell him about my parents, Cy Gabriel, the Project, the Presence, the derm on the nurse's neck, but the new, more powerful me was gripped by the certainty that confiding in Gip would be a terrible mistake.

I was part of a new and greater team.

When I returned to the house, I found Amy in the sitting-room watching TV. I sat down beside her, my mind still teeming with thoughts of my conversation with Gip.

"How's the old Project going these days?" I asked as casually as I could manage.

"Fine."

"Any hot news from the Presence?"

"It's not a joke, Thomas. There has been nothing more serious than this in the history of humankind."

We watched the TV in silence. Some sad game show was

on. As the latest member of the audience was brought on stage to giggle and gasp and blush as they competed for a holiday somewhere or other, it occurred to me that, for all humankind's faults, it was at least human.

I laughed loudly at some pathetic joke the show's host had made. My sister looked at me, surprised.

"What's the matter? Don't they do jokes where you come from?" I asked. "You'd think they would make humor part of the Project."

Amy turned to me. "You just don't get it, do you?" she said. "Mum and Dad and me have the same sort of emotions as you have. We feel what you feel."

"So why don't you want to talk about it?"

Amy returned to the screen. "Doesn't matter," she murmured.

Every fiber of my being seemed to be telling me to leave it there. All is good, all will be resolved. But the person I had once been could not be ignored. I thought of Rendle, of the nurse. If the Project was looking after Rendle's mother, who was to say the Project had not killed him? And, if angels could remove an innocent math teacher, who else was in danger? "What happens if something goes wrong?" I asked Amy.

"Wrong?"

"Yeah. Say someone found out about the Project and didn't fancy being saved."

Amy sighed a weary, big-sister sigh. "Won't happen," she said. "We're not stupid. It's all been worked out."

"But if it did. What would happen if a person found some kind of secret file, say, and put the Project in danger?"

"You're out of your depth, Tom." Amy looked at me and I noticed that blotches of color had appeared on her cheekbones, like when I had asked her about a boyfriend when she was younger. "Leave it, OK?"

I sat back. "I guess you'd just nix the guy, right?"

"Nix." Laughing unconvincingly, Amy shook her head. "You know, you can be just so childish sometimes."

"Sorry," I shrugged. "I'm only human. Unlike some people round here."

Amy took a deep breath as if to keep herself in check. "The Project comes first," she said quietly. She turned to look at me, and I could have sworn that there was warning, even threat in her eyes. "Just remember that. The Project comes first."

I sat back and watched the TV. Her answer had told me all I needed to know.

After supper that night, I called Gip.

"That stuff about my real mother," I said. "Were you serious about helping me find her?"

Gip laughed, a hard, unfriendly sound. "Good old Tom," he said. "I knew you'd come around."

"I'm just asking."

"We can get up to Norfolk tomorrow if you like."

"Gip, I'm not sure. Anyway, I haven't got any money."

"Don't worry about money. 8:30? After your parents have gone to work?"

"Can I think about it?"

"Nope. 8:30, it is. We're off to Cromer."

"My real mum."

"Yeah. Tom's going home. It's time."

22 · MIRACULO

WHEN GIP HAD A PROJECT, there was no shifting him. The next morning, at 8:30 precisely, he was there on my doorstep. I pleaded that I was feeling ill but he told me that he had paid his friend Manny to take us up to Norfolk. By the time he had led me down the street to where there sat a tall, black, dreadlocked guy, eyes closed and apparently asleep, in the driver's seat of his bright red, heavily dented Golf, there was no going back.

I climbed in the back. A few grunted introductions were made. At some point, Manny revealed that, since he had bought his car, he had been stopped by the police seventeen times. He had shaken his head as if he still couldn't believe that such a thing could happen. "It's racism, man," he muttered.

Right now, as we took the motorway out of London, I was praying for that eighteenth time. Manny's car seemed to have a powerful engine but no exhaust so that, as we barreled up the fast lane of a dual carriageway, we made a noise like an angry chainsaw accompanied by the thump of the stereo. I sat slumped gloomily in the back, feeling like a kidnap victim and wishing I had stayed in bed.

As we headed east, I gazed out of the window at the parched gold-yellow stubble fields and wondered how all this was happening to me. Where had Gip found the money to pay Manny? How did these two know each other? What were we going to do once we reached this Cromer place? I felt guilty about my parents, about Cy. Apart from the small matter of not telling me that I had been adopted, they had been fair and open with me. Now, in return, I was on some crazy hunt for my real mother. I hadn't even left them a note.

It took us near on three hours to reach Cromer, which turned out to be an old-fashioned seaside town full of fairgrounds, ice cream vans and families wandering about in a bored, happy, holiday kind of way. Manny found a car park overlooking a pebbly beach and switched off the engine. For a few moments, we sat there, our ears ringing from the effects of rap and chainsaw.

"What a dump," Gip said eventually.

"Eh?" Manny looked across at him, surprised. "This is great, here." He stepped out of the car, stretched his long arms skyward and for the first time I realized just how tall and broad-shouldered he was. As he gazed towards the beach, the breeze catching his long hair, he looked like a giant of the deep who had just emerged from the waves to claim his kingdom. "Sea air," he said. "Just the ticket, man."

Gip and I got out of the car. "Manny used to work for some debt collection agency," he said. "He knows how to track people down, get them to talk."

"What, you were like a sort of private detective?" I asked.

"Yeah." Manny looked out to sea and seemed almost embarrassed. "Find the loser, remind him that he was behind with his payments, that sort of thing."

"And then, like, frighten him up a bit, right?" Gip laughed.

"Didn't like it." Manny shook his head. "They fired me when they discovered that I was pretending I couldn't find people. I felt sorry for them, man."

A middle-aged man, all dark glasses, Bermuda shorts and beer gut, was passing by.

"Excuse me," Manny spoke in a surprisingly genteel voice. "I was wondering if you could tell us where the post office was."

The man looked up nervously. "Post office?"

Manny smiled. "We've just arrived, you see."

Glancing suspiciously at Gip and me, the man pointed towards the town. "Tucker Street," he said. "Behind the church." He hurried on.

Manny, it was true, knew a bit about the person-finding business. At Cromer Post Office, we borrowed a telephone directory. There were about a hundred Garnhams in its pages but only about ten were listed with a local number. Of those, two had the initial "K."

Gip handed me his mobile phone.

I was about to make some excuse but Gip had turned away. "We're getting some ice cream," he said. "We'll catch you in ten."

I sat on a chair nearby, gazing at the phone in my hand. There was no way out. Gip had paid for this trip. Manny had spent a day of his life driving to this weird little town. Now it was my turn.

I dialed. The voice of an ancient woman answered. I explained that I was looking for Karen Garnham. She told me her name was Thea, then she started telling me about a million of her relatives, none of whom were called Karen. Before I got the full Garnham family history, I said goodbye and hung up.

The second number was the answering machine of a Ken Garnham. Relieved, I stood in the cubicle, looking around for Gip and Manny. I had done my best but, face it, the chance of finding my mum when every other person around here seemed to be called Garnham was pretty hopeless. Shame about that; let's go home.

But there was no sign of them. After a couple of minutes, I decided to take the telephone book back to the Post Office counter. I was just about to close the page when the name "NK Garnham" caught my eye. My heart beat faster. Some inexplicable instinct told me that this was the number that would lead to my mother.

I picked up the receiver and dialed.

A man answered. "Is Karen Garnham there, please?" I asked. My voice sounded odd and trembly as if I was suddenly a frightened little boy.

"Down the pier," said the man.

I closed my eyes and took a couple of deep breaths. When I spoke again, I had to force the words out. "Where would she be on the pier, please?" I asked.

"Usual place, on stage." The man sounded irritated. "Prancing about in a swimsuit in the end of the pier show." He hesitated. "Who is this?"

"My name's Thomas Wisdom. I need to see Karen Garnham on a matter of urgency."

The man grunted impatiently. "Now what's she been up to, then?"

"Nothing," I said quickly. "What time will Karen be . . . on stage?"

"Whenever that prat of a magician's on."

"Fine. Thanks."

"Oh, and she's not called Karen, by the way. Her professional stage name is Maria Procchutti." He chuckled. "Silly cow," he added almost to himself.

I thanked him and put the telephone down carefully. On stage. In a swimsuit. Maria Procchutti. What exactly had I let myself in for?

I stood there thinking for a moment. When I looked up, I realized that Gip and Manny had returned and were watching me. I closed the telephone book.

"We're in business," I said.

As we made our way down to the pier, people stared at us as if seeing a couple of small white blokes walking on either side of a Rastafarian twice their size was a rare sight in these parts.

"What's the matter with these people?" Gip muttered at one point.

"Racism, man," said Manny without any particular bitterness. After a while, he took to greeting passers-by.

"Good afternoon," he would say in a chipper, gentlemanly accent. "Lovely day, isn't it?" Children giggled at him but their parents hurried by as if even Manny's smiles were a danger to their little ones.

I had expected Cromer Pier to be a giant platform, jutting into the sea, full of sideshows and merry-go-rounds but it turned out to be little more than a hundred yards long with a single, ramshackle building at the end. Across the entrance, there hung a giant streamer reading *Fun for all the Family at Cromer's Famous SEASIDE SPECIAL!*

We joined the queue at the box-office. When we reached the front, the old woman selling tickets told us, with some satisfaction, that the matinée performance was sold out. A few tickets were left for the evening show. "We'll have three," said Gip, pulling £30 from his wallet as if he had money to burn.

"I'll pay you back," I said as he handed me my ticket.

"Course you will," said Gip.

The sun was shining, we were by the seaside, we had time on our hands but I wasn't in the mood for fun.

I went along with Gip and Manny, had a hot dog, watched them as they shared a bumper car, played a round of crazy golf. At some point, I rang home and left a message on the answering-machine, telling my parents not to worry, that I was safe with Gip, that I would be home tomorrow. As evening approached, we sat on the beach, staring out to sea, now and then chucking stones into the waves.

Nearby, parents were packing up their things, gathering their children after another tough day on the beach in Cromer. All day, it had been as if Cy Gabriel had never spoken to me, as if angels were nothing more scary than something you sang about at Christmastime.

I looked about me. Did these people—that bony, white-skinned dad in a floppy hat, that overweight mum wiping the ice cream off her little boy's mouth, those boys kicking a beach ball—really need saving? I thought of what had happened that day, of Gip setting up this trip, of Manny and his smile, even of the grumpy old girl in the box-office. Was all this so bad that it needed to be transformed by a great Project to make us all better people?

"All right then, Tom?" Gip lay on his back with his eyes closed. There was sand in his hair and a smear of chocolate ice cream had dried on his chin.

"Nervous," I said. "I'm not so sure this was such a great idea."

Gip sat up, drew his knees up to his chin and stared out to sea. "When Dover told me where your real mum lived, I thought about not telling you. Maybe things were stirred up enough in your life. Family stuff usually means trouble, as far as I can see."

"So what made you change your mind?"

"I put myself in your shoes. Would I want to meet my real mum? Of course I would. Knowing there was some stranger out there who had brought me into the world would be like a missing part of the jigsaw. I'd want to meet her, just so that I could get on with the rest of my life."

I nodded, knowing that Gip was right as usual. "Ever since I discovered that I was adopted, I've been wondering what she's like," I said. "I keep drifting into this fantasy—as if she's this perfect, older friend who understands me better than anyone else because we share the same blood. We'd meet and suddenly, by magic, I'd lose this feeling that I'm an outsider in the world. I'd belong at last."

Gip picked up a stone and threw it as far as he could. I watched it splash into the sea.

"Now I'm here, I realize how crazy that idea was," I said. "She's a stranger, leading her own life. She could be any woman on this beach and I wouldn't know any better. Just because I was once part of her won't make any difference at all."

"She'll be all right, mark my words," said Gip. "Face it, she can't be that bad—look at the way you've turned out."

"I wish I was on my own here."

Gip looked at me and smiled. "I know you do. But sometimes you need your friends—you can rely on your mates better than on any family."

Manny stood up. "It's showtime," he said and began trudging across the pebbles towards the pier.

I sat for a moment, reluctant to move. Meeting my real mum would be tough enough, but seeing her on stage in front of hundreds of people, including my own best friend, seemed a special kind of torture.

"Coming?" Gip asked.

"I want to go home," I murmured.

Gip nodded in the direction of Manny who was still striding across the beach. "Want to try and stop him?" he said.

Sighing, I stood up. Gip was right. It was too late to turn back.

We joined the people who were streaming into the theater on the pier, laughing and joking, ready for the show. Our seats were near the front and to the side which was kind of lucky since anyone sitting behind Manny would have seen nothing but his big dreadlocked head.

I remember little of the first half of the show. There were dancers who kicked up their legs and stared with fixed smiles beyond the back of the auditorium as if gazing at a brighter, better future than a Seaside Special in Cromer. The compère, a gray-haired guy with a Liverpool accent and a permanently startled expression on his face, introduced each act with a string of jokes. A dodgy-looking bloke with an Italian accent sang some old-fashioned songs. A family of jugglers threw stuff around the stage.

The audience loved it and, to tell the truth, I would have too were it not for the fact that I was just about to see my mother for the first time since I was a baby. Now and then I glanced to my left, where Gip was taking it all in with the cool lack of enthusiasm he showed in geography lessons. Manny, on my other side, was having the time of his life, guffawing so loudly at the jokes that nearby members of the audience soon began laughing at his laughter.

"Easy, Manny," I muttered after one particularly embarrassing and lengthy thunderclap. He looked across at me, eyes shining with pleasure. "This is so great, man," he said loudly.

And then it happened. The compère was introducing the Great Miraculo and his lovely assistant Maria. A couple of stage assistants brought a long table on to the stage. A man with a ridiculous top hat and a silly mustache wandered on to tumultuous applause. Behind him, wobbling on high heels, was a woman in a shiny blonde wig, wearing—or almost wearing—a swimsuit and fishnet tights.

"Oh no." I actually said these words out loud. "Please no."

Gip lay a hand on my arm. I recoiled, covering my face with both hands.

I saw little of the act. Every time I dared to look, the Miraculo guy seemed to be getting a laugh at my mother's expense. He dropped a handkerchief and leered at her as she picked it up. He followed her about and suddenly a white rabbit appeared out of his trouser pocket. He put her in a box on stage and set about sawing her in half but—big joke—he couldn't get the saw through her stomach.

I was never expecting this. The Great Miraculo was not so much a magician as a lame comic turn whose biggest joke was that his assistant—my poor, sad mother—was a bit too big to be wobbling about in a swimsuit.

Gip and I sat in silence as the audience, including Manny, rocked with laughter. Towards the end, I lowered my hands from my face, ignored the nightmare magician and stared into the face of my mother, the "lovely Maria."

Her smile, beneath the absurd blonde wig, never faltered. As the audience cheered and laughed, she gazed out at us with unseeing eyes like some overweight doll. When, after what seemed like an age, she tottered off the stage, followed by the Great Miraculo, who was still leering at her bottom, I found that I was damp with sweat.

"She was great, your mum." Chuckling, Manny shook his head. "Best act of the show, that was."

"Thanks a lot," I muttered.

"All right?" Gip smiled at me.

"Let's get out of here," I said.

But there were three or four more acts before the Seaside Special reached its climax. I sat there, numbed and silent, feeling like a freak among the happy families, a black hole of misery in the light and laughter. It seemed to me that my mood was reaching the people who were sitting close to me—not just Gip, or Manny, who was suddenly silent, but the family behind us. It was if they all could sense that in their midst was a boy who had just seen his mother for the first time for twelve years to discover that she was fat, with too much make-up, a joke bimbo in a seaside show.

She came on once again, for the final curtain-call. As she stepped forward to take her bow, she smiled up at the kinky-mustached magician, then at us, and, just for a split second, I thought I caught a glimpse of the real person behind the mask. Then the curtain fell and it was all over.

When we emerged onto the pier, it was almost dark. Frankly I wanted to forget what I had just seen. I began walking in the direction of the car.

"Hang on, Tom." Gip hobbled along, half a step behind me. "Is that it?"

"Yeah." I kept going. "I've seen all I need to see."

"You've seen your mum at work. You haven't even talked to her."

I laughed bitterly and shook my head. "Forget it," I muttered.

I felt a hand on my shoulder. It was Manny.

"We ain't traveled across half the country to watch you run away." He strengthened his grip alarmingly. "So you've got a bit of a crazy mama. Welcome to the club, man." He reached into his back pocket and pulled out a scrap of paper. "Besides, I want her autograph. I thought she was dead good."

Run away. It was those words that kept me from walking on. I knew that if I left it there, headed back to London, that image of my mother—pale, lit-up by the lights, spilling hopelessly out of her swimsuit—would be with me for the rest of my life. It made me sad—for me and for her.

I took the slip of paper. "Got a pen?" I asked Gip.

He reached into his jeans and passed me a ballpoint pen. "There you go, Tom." He smiled—one of those big Gip grins that are special because they are so rare. "We'll wait here for you."

I walked back to the gates of the theater and asked a man in a uniform where I might get the autographs of the stars of the Seaside Special. He looked at me suspiciously for a moment, then pointed to a dark passage down one side of the pier. "Towards the life-boat slip," he said. "They'll be coming out soon."

I made my way to the end of the passage. There I stood in the half-light, watching a small door with a green light over it, listening to the sound of the waves and the distant music, waiting for my mother.

23 · CHARMER

AFTER ABOUT FIVE MINUTES, the door opened. Against the lights from inside, I saw the outline of three figures. As they walked towards me, I recognized two of the dancers and the smoothie singer. The girls glanced at me, half-curious, but the guy stared ahead, chatting away. I guess that, since he was wearing dark glasses and it was almost dark, he didn't even see me.

The juggling family were next, all five of them. Then the compère who looked kind of old and lost now that he was back in the real world. Then three more dancers. "All right, love?" asked one.

"I'm waiting for Maria—Karen, that is."

"Yeah?" The dancer hesitated and I thought I saw a look of concern cross her face. "Friend of hers, are you?"

"I . . . I just want her autograph."

One of the other dancers muttered something in the ear of her friend. "Shut up, Steph," said the woman who had talked to me. "Would you like me to—?" The door opened again. "Well, talk of the devil," she said.

I turned. My mother stood in the doorway, her hand over the arm of the Great Miraculo. "Can I help you?" she said in a tone that was not exactly friendly.

"Could I have your autograph, please?"

"Sure." The magician stepped forward, reaching inside his jacket and taking out a pen.

"Not yours," I said quickly. "Karen's."

"Cheeky little devil." The man brushed past me. "Get on with it, love," he called over his shoulder. "I'm gasping for a pint."

My mother stood motionless. Something about my voice, my presence here, seemed to have alarmed her. "How did you know my real name?" she asked.

"I rang your home. The person who answered said you'd be here."

"That bloomin' bloke of yours." Miraculo stood about five yards away. "Never could keep his mouth shut."

"My home." My mother stepped forward and the lights from the pier caught her face. Without her blonde wig and wearing clothes, she looked more normal and younger than she had seemed on stage. "What's going on?"

"I'm a fan," I said, passing her the piece of paper and the ballpoint pen.

"Bit young for you, love." Miraculo laughed harshly behind me.

My mother signed and gave me the piece of paper. On it was written "Maria Procchutti" with three kisses and a heart. "Don't listen to him, love." She winked at me. "He's only jealous."

She was about to step past me and disappear out of my life forever. There was no time for second thoughts. I said the words in a low, firm voice that only she could hear.

"You're my mother. I'm your son."

The expression on her face changed, hardened, almost as if I had just insulted her. "What did you say?"

"Twelve years ago, you had me adopted. My name was Michael."

I had been imagining this moment. In my mind, I had seen my mother taking me in her arms, maybe crying a bit. But now, in real life, she stepped back. "Who put you up to this?" she asked, her eyes wide with alarm.

"I just wanted to see you."

Miraculo moved closer. "What's all this about? What you up to, sonny?"

"He's just having a bit of laugh, love." My mother glared at me, daring me to contradict her. "Nothing to worry about. He's got his autograph. Let's—"

"Please!" For the first time, there was a crack in my voice. "I've come all the way from London."

Miraculo stepped between me and my mother. Leaning forward towards me, his hands on his knees, "D'you know what they do to troublemakers round here? They pick them up and then they chuck them in the drink." He straightened up, took my mother by the arm and began to walk away. "Get lost, sonny," he said loudly. "Or I'll have to call Security."

"Security's here." It was the deep, unmistakable voice of Manny, who stood, arms crossed, blocking their exit. "That's my friend and he wants to talk to her," he said with polite menace. "And that's what he's going to do."

"You . . . you reckon, do ya?" Miraculo was unable to keep the fear out of his voice.

"I do."

"Are you threatening me?" Miraculo tried for a laugh but it sounded more like a wimper.

"Absolutely not." Manny looked shocked. "I'm just explaining. Making things clear."

My mother extricated her arm from Miraculo's. "Go to the pub, Brian," she said quietly. "I'll catch you later."

The magician hesitated. "I can't leave you here with this—" he glanced up at Manny, "this goon."

"Don't worry," said Manny in his most friendly manner. "We'll keep you company."

"Go on, love," said my mother. "I'll be all right."

I watched the Great Miraculo make his way down the pier, followed by Manny and Gip. My mother turned back to me and crossed her arms disapprovingly, looking for the first time like a real parent. "Nice friends you've got there," she said sarcastically.

"The best," I said.

"How about you telling me what this is all about?"

"That's all I want to do."

"Let's find somewhere where we can talk," she said, and began walking down the pier.

My mother and I sat on a bench looking out over the gray, dark sea. She lit a cigarette.

"What did you think of the act?" she asked after a few moments' uneasy silence.

"I thought it was good," I lied.

"We get some laughs, eh."

"Yeah." I thought of the blonde wig, the high heels, the tight, glittering swimsuit. "You certainly do."

"We've got a pantomime gig in Ipswich this year. There's talk of Blackpool next summer." She inhaled on her cigarette, then turned to look at me. "What about you?" she asked.

"I'm still at school."

"Tell me about yourself."

I told her. I spoke about my life with Mark and Mary Wisdom. I said we had a nice home in the suburbs. I was doing pretty well in my class, that I hoped to be in the football team for my year. I even mentioned Dougal. The more I spoke, the smaller and more predictable it all seemed.

Yet, by the way she gazed at me while I was talking, I might have been telling her how I was the youngest ever recipient of the Nobel Peace Prize. "My son," she said when I stopped talking. "I always knew you'd do well for yourself. Looks like I made the right choice, doesn't it?"

"Giving me away, you mean."

She chuckled to herself. "You've got to admit that you're better off where you are than tagging along after a magician's assistant."

"Maybe—"

"Oh, I know it might seem glamorous to you, the showbiz life, but it's no way to bring up a kid."

"It doesn't seem that—" I was about to say that her life had not struck me as being exactly glamorous but I thought better of it. "It doesn't seem too bad," I said.

She smiled. "You're very kind," she said. As if realizing that these words were a bit formal, considering the fact that she was my long-lost mother, she laid a cold hand on mine. I looked down at her long, curling fingernails. They looked like painted claws. I took my hand away.

"Why did you do it?" I asked.

She sat in silence for a while, then sighed. "I think I was always too selfish to be a mum. I never got on with kids, even when I was one myself. Anyway, I can hardly look after myself, let alone someone else."

I asked who my father was.

She winced like someone pretending to be embarrassed. "I was a bit of a tearaway when I was a teenager. I got into trouble at school and had a baby boy. The social took him away from me. After that I ran a bit wild. You came along when I was eighteen. I'd been seeing this bloke who ran a pub in North Walsham." She stared out to sea, lost in memory. "He was a bit married, so I had no choice but adoption. I didn't like it at the time but there wasn't much I could do—I weren't much more than a kid myself."

"A bloke who ran a pub," I murmured. "Great."

"He was nice—a real charmer, like you. I heard that his business went under and that he's gone down to the West country. Haven't heard from him for years."

"Are you married now?"

She shook her head. "I've lived with this bloke for a couple of years but, between you and me, it's not too clever between us right now. When Brian—that's Miraculo—gets his divorce, we'll probably get it together. We're all right, Brian and me."

And, quite suddenly, there didn't seem much more to say. There we were, mother and son, together at last. Yet, with every word we spoke to one another, the gulf between us seemed greater.

"Thank you for finding me." My mother took my hand again and this time I didn't move away. "Your dad was a weak man but I can tell that you're different. It's good that we've met at last."

I smiled. "It is," I said, and I meant it.

She looked at me for a moment. Then, without warning, she put her arms around me and pulled me close to her. The smell of tobacco and perfume on her coat was over-powering but I leaned against her without resisting. "Little Michael," she murmured. "You're a good kid."

She reached into the white leather bag that was on the bench beside her and took out a card. On it, in large, fancy letters, were written the words, The Great Miraculo (and his lovely assistant Maria Procchutti) Comedy and Magic! Underneath was written an address and a telephone number.

"Listen, I know I've been a bad mother and all that but, if you're ever in trouble, you can reach me here at any time," she said. "I'm not much good at relationships but I'd like to make it up to you somehow."

I stood up. "Thanks . . . Mum."

She laughed. "Don't," she said. "You make me feel so old. I think I'd better be Karen, don't you?"

I nodded. "And I'm not Michael. I'm Thomas—Thomas Wisdom."

We smiled at each other. Then she folded her arms and shivered. "Off you go then, Thomas Wisdom," she said softly.

I turned and walked towards the lights of Cromer. Gip and Manny were waiting for me by the car. We drove home in silence.

It was almost two in the morning by the time we reached London and Manny dropped us off at the squat and drove off to some private destination of his own. We made our way upstairs. As usual, the room next to the motorway was empty. We crashed out on a bed in the corner, huddling together under a thin blanket.

The roar of early-morning traffic awoke me. I lay on my side looking, beyond Gip's sleeping form, to the hazy brightness outside. My head ached, my body felt grimy. I longed to be able to get up, have a bath and clean my teeth in a neat, suburban bathroom and put on some fresh clothes. I realized that, unlike Gip, I was not one of life's natural squatters.

Something else. I thought of my mother, sitting there at the end of the bench, her hard, dark eyes staring out to sea, now and then putting a cigarette to her lips and drawing on it like it was a life-support machine. I remembered the smell on her coat. Then I thought of my other parents, Mark and Mary, and my sister Amy. I saw my home, my room, my crazy dog asleep on my bed.

Yesterday I had faced it all, my past and my present. I had stood up and walked away, no longer just somebody's son, a name on adoption papers, part of the Project, but me. No one was going to decide my future for me. I was free. I was strong. The time for secrets was over.

I prodded Gip. He swore at me. I sat up in bed, shook him by the shoulder. He turned over, blinking at the brightness.

"I've got something to tell you," I said.

"Eh?"

"It's called the Project . . ."

24 · CHAT

WITHIN HALF A NANO-SECOND of my entering my house the next morning, my parents were in the hall. They stood staring at me, as if unable quite to believe that I was there, and then my mother said "Thomas" in a voice that was gentle yet exasperated. She walked towards me and took me in her arms.

I glanced over her shoulder at my father. He seemed to have aged overnight.

"I think you owe us an explanation, old boy," he said.

"I told you. I went to look for my real mother. She turned out to be really nice."

My other mother, Mary Wisdom, released me and stood back. "You found her?"

"Of course. She's a brilliant magician. We're going to keep in touch. It's going to be great."

At that moment, voices could be heard coming from the sitting-room.

"There's a meeting going on," said my father.

At any other time, I might have noticed how strange this was but at that moment my only idea was to get away, to soak in a bath upstairs.

"We'd like you to join us," said my mother.

Now I was curious. I followed them into the sitting-room.

Three men were there, two of whom I knew. Sitting in front of the window was Cy Gabriel. Nearby on the sofa, in trim weekend clothes, was Daisy Dover, headmaster of my school. Beside him sat a tall man in his late thirties. He was wearing a police uniform.

"You know everyone except Chief Superintendent Wilson," said my mother as if we were at a neighborhood sherry party.

The policeman stood up, put the peaked cap that had been on his lap under his arm, and shook my hand.

"Glad to meet you at last, Thomas," he said in a gruff, leader-of-men voice.

"How do you do," I muttered.

"Take a seat, Thomas." My father smiled. I sat in the one remaining empty chair, feeling like the accused in a court of law.

"Things have kind of moved on since we discussed the Project at the office." It was Cy Gabriel who spoke.

I frowned. "I thought that was meant to be a big secret."

"It is."

I looked around the room, slowly coming to terms with what I was hearing. "You mean you're all—"

Cy smiled in a manner that he presumably meant to be reassuring. "We're angels, yes."

"Ah. Fine." I tried to keep the astonishment out of my voice but the fact was that, of all the people I knew, Daisy

Dover was the least angelic. He smiled at me now, thinly and insincerely, as if reading my thoughts.

"We're active pretty much everywhere," Cy was saying. "In schools. In the police force. In the media. In government. The Project is going very, very well."

"Great."

"We're now entering a new phase. What we call 'integration.' The next generation of indigenous humans is about to be introduced to the Project. All over the world children are being raised or educated by angels. Sometimes they are adopted. Sometimes we reach them at an early age with what we call 'mentors.'"

"What are—?"

"You remember when you were three or four. You had an imaginary friend, right?"

I shrugged, embarrassed by the memory. There was this guy, Ricky, who used to be there all day. He was the person I told everything to. Once or twice I had insisted that my mother laid a place at the table for Ricky. It was something of a family joke because, of course, Ricky belonged in my imagination. Or so I thought.

"He was a mentor," said Cy. "He was providing you with preparatory information about the Project."

I shook my head. "Are you telling me that all those imaginary friends children all over the world are talking to are not imaginary at all but little brainwashing mentors?"

"Brainwashing's the wrong word." Cy shook his head with the merest hint of irritation. "It's more like informal education. We're also getting through to other kids through certain computers. They don't know it but, every time they stare at that screen, they're learning about the path of goodness. One day, they will be the people to save the planet."

"So that was why I was given a computer—to give the Project a shortcut into my brain." I glanced at my parents. They were both staring at the floor.

"You guys, the adopted—you're the ones who matter right now," Cy continued. "You've got the knowledge. We have put our trust in you. All we need is for you is to put your trust in us in return."

The semi-circle of angels looked at me as if expecting me to say something, maybe to express my gratitude, but right then I was still annoyed about the computer. If Mum and Dad were prepared to let my mind be messed up by encouraging me to look at a screen, what else would they be prepared to do on behalf of the famous Project?

"You are prepared to put your trust in us, aren't you, Thomas?" Dad spoke and his words seemed more a statement than a question.

"I don't quite get it," I said. "If I hadn't hacked into your computer and then followed you and Mum in California, I'd still know nothing about all this."

My father glanced across at his boss and, in that moment, I sensed that more worrying news was on the way.

"Tom, those things weren't accidents," said Cy. "The Project was guiding you."

I frowned, at first unable to take in what I was being told. "I was set up," I whispered.

"We presented you with a few little tests. You passed them all—admittedly with the help of your friend Gary Sanchez. At that moment we knew you were worthy of our trust."

"Thanks." A sudden thought had occurred to me. "So where does that leave Gip?"

It was the headteacher Daisy Dover who sat forward at this point. "As you may know, Gary got in touch with me last week concerning the tragic accident that took Colin Rendle from us. He told me about your visit to his house, how you had certain suspicions concerning the nurse who is looking after Mrs. Rendle. He's a bright lad, Gary, but I rather fear that he's getting into something he doesn't understand. The first thing we need to know is if he has any knowledge of the Project."

"No." The lie tripped off my tongue with surprising ease. "If I told him, he'd think I had gone crazy."

"We'd like him on board." Cy spoke casually. "We need people of his caliber on our team."

"Gip was never exactly into teams."

"But first—" Cy smiled as if I were his greatest friend in the world. "First we need to find him."

The police guy, Wilson, stirred into life. "Our information is that Gary has not been living at home for the last week or two."

He looked at me expectantly. I said nothing.

"He must have some other hideout."

I shrugged. "He's always been a bit mysterious about that," I said.

This time no one believed me.

"I wish I could convey to you how important this is," said Cy in the voice of a teacher severely disappointed by your behavior. "Important for the Project, of course. But really important for Gary too."

There was something about that word "important" which worried me. It was like "good" and "helpful." When angels spoke, there was a hint of threat in the most innocent words. I realized that I had to say something to throw them off the track for a while, to give us some time.

"Maybe I could bring him here," I said. "We could tell him about the Project together."

I sensed relief in the room.

"That would be so great, Thomas," said Cy. "Could you do that for us?"

"No promises," I said. "But I could try."

I was bushed. After the meeting broke up, I lolled about in my room for a while. My parents went to work and I cooked myself a fry-up for lunch. I watched some TV. I did not look at my computer. Mum and Dad came home together at about six, almost as if nothing had happened. Over an early-evening dinner, my father casually asked me if I had spoken to Gary. I said Gip seemed not to be at home. After I had eaten, I went upstairs, fell into bed, and crashed out.

I awoke sharply, as if my unconscious mind had heard something. The house was dark and silent. It was half-past one. I got up, slipped into my clothes and silently let myself out of the house.

I made my way to the bus stop. There was a night bus route which seemed to be heading in the right direction for Gip's squat and I was in luck—a bus rumbled around the corner like some nocturnal beast and pulled up beside me.

The driver glanced at me like twelve-year-olds were always getting on his bus in the early hours of the morning. I asked him if he could tell me when we reached my stop. He shrugged his agreement.

On the backseat, a man with a heavy, matted beard lay stretched out, eyes closed, with a beer can in his hand. I sat near the front.

London was a different city at this time of night. People scurried like rats along the neon-lit streets. Now and then I would spot a figure huddled asleep in the entrance of a shop or a couple of people standing in the shadows, watching, waiting for someone or something. Beardo on the back-seat began singing a sort of football chant, again and again. Once he sat up and shouted something at me. I sat tight and ignored him. He swore at me and then seemed to go back to sleep.

After about half an hour, the driver mumbled something. I stepped off the bus.

I looked around me and realized that I was in luck—the street where I stood was the one Gip and I had walked down several times over the past few weeks. Head down, hands in pockets, I headed for the squat.

I turned into the row of condemned houses. It was dark here, unlit even by street lamps, and the buildings on each side of me seemed more bleak and threatening than they had in the daytime.

The house that was Gip's secret hideout showed no sign of life. I rang the bell, again and again. After about five minutes, a girl's voice could be heard on the other side of the door. "Who is it?" she called out.

"It's Thomas. Gip's friend."

The door opened slightly and, in the darkness, I saw the pale face of the girl I had seen in the kitchen the first time I had been here. With a wary look to check that I was alone, she stepped back to let me in. I saw now that she was carrying a candle.

"They cut off the power," she said, heading up the stairs. We reached the first floor. "You'll find him in his room," she said, nodding in the direction of the next flight of stairs before she disappeared into her room, leaving me in the pitch black of the corridor.

I groped my way upstairs and along the corridor until I reached the last door on the left. I knocked once. There was no reply. I opened the door.

Gip was awake. He was sitting on a stool, his back to the door, silhouetted by the glow of his laptop screen.

"Gip," I hissed.

He turned. Few things can startle Gip Sanchez and my appearing at his secret hideout in the middle of the night was not one of them. "How you doing?"

"We've got to talk," I said. I walked over to the window, the lights of cars on the motorway flashed by like meteors across the sky.

Gip switched off his laptop.

"I thought they cut the power," I said.

"Battery." There was a hint of chilly impatience in Gip's voice.

"I found out something about computers today. Angels sometimes use them to brainwash people about the Project."

"Not mine, mate." The voice came back through the semi-darkness. "No one knows I've got it. I'm as invisible on-line as I am in this room. Was that what you crossed London to tell me?"

"Daisy's an angel."

Now I had his attention. "You're kidding," he said.

"There was this meeting at my house today. Dover was there, and Cy Gabriel and some bloke from the police. They want you to join the Project. They've been looking all over for you. They asked me to bring you to them."

"Why me?"

"They seem to think you're their kind of guy. I guess they'd prefer you to be on their side."

"Did you tell them I knew about the Project?"

"Somehow that didn't seem a great idea."

"I'm in trouble," Gip murmured as if he were talking to himself. "First Rendle. Now me."

"What's Rendle got to do with this?"

"I've worked out why they killed him. Your parents were going to tell you about the Project at some stage, right?"

I nodded.

"But we kind of messed up their plans. We found your file on your dad's computer. They must have thought that would be no problem—after all, it was in this unbreakable code. But then we gave it to Colin Rendle. Big mistake. If he was just an ordinary math teacher, there was no way that he would have been able to do anything with it. But he wasn't. He happens to be this secret mathematical genius. He cracks the code and that's where everything starts going wrong. You find out you're adopted. Rendle speaks to Daisy. At that point, the angel guys must have thought that, if he had cracked that file, he must have access to all sorts of other stuff about the Project."

"Exit Rendle."

"Right. He knew too much for his own good."

"But they're always saying that the Project is meant to be the power of goodness on Earth."

"Yeah." Gip laughed bitterly. "Some angels."

We sat in silence for a moment. "So what are you going to do?" I asked.

"They want me to join the Project. That either means I get to help them save the world or some nasty little accident takes me out of the equation. To tell the truth, I'm not tempted either way."

"If you just stay here, they won't find you. You're safe while the holiday lasts. But what happens when term starts and you're not at school?"

"Maybe the Project will have moved on by then." Outside a car flashed by, lighting up Gip's face for an instant. I sensed that he was feeling less confident about his future than he was letting on. "I've been on-line today," he said suddenly.

"Yeah?"

"There are loads of chatrooms for kids, you know."

"And?"

"I've found one or two rooms and newsgroups that are particularly for adopted kids. So I've been doing a bit of research."

I hate it when Gip does this. He lets information out bit by bit, as if he's reluctant to let it go. "Research," I repeated wearily.

"Yeah. I've been asking adopted kids all over the world to look out for some tell-tale signs about their adoptive parents. Birthmarks on their necks and arms. Co-ordinated visits to the lavatory. Visits to California. Peculiar behavior, generally."

I couldn't believe what I was hearing. "What is it with you?" I said. "You've blown the whole thing."

"I was just curious." He turned back to the computer and pressed a button on the side console. "I wanted to know how serious this famous Project is."

"So what did you find out?" I went over and stood beside him in front of the screen.

Gip moved the mouse and double-clicked. A message appeared in the left-hand corner of the screen. It read, You have 437 messages.

"Looks like it's pretty serious," he said. He laughed briefly but his eyes, lit up by the glow of the computer screen, betrayed him.

Gip was scared.

I was back home before breakfast, my head throbbing with sleeplessness. Dumping my clothes in a heap on the floor, I tumbled into bed.

Although all I wanted to do was sleep, my mind was humming with the events of the last twelve hours. Gip was in danger. As if that was not bad enough, he was contacting people across the world who might be in the same situation as me. Until now I had managed to persuade myself that the events of the past few weeks were all about me. Now there was no escaping the fact that my little family crisis was part of a bigger, more frightening picture.

At some point, as I lay there thinking about all this, the door opened softly. My mother looked at me. Seeing that I was awake, she came over and sat on my bed.

"How did you sleep?" she asked softly.

"Good," I lied.

She laid a cool hand on my brow. "Don't worry about all this," she said. "We'll be back to normal soon."

"Yeah, right."

"Our own little family. Just like before."

I rolled on to my back and looked up at her. Was she serious, I wondered. What was more important for her— being an angel, part of the great universal Project to save poor little Planet Earth, or the fact that she was my mum?

"You know I love you very much," she said, as if she could read my thoughts.

I grunted, kind of embarrassed.

"An angel's love is the best." She smoothed the hair out of my face.

"Out of this world."

She nodded, smiling.

"What happens if Gip doesn't want to join the Project?" I asked.

"He will. I know I've never been too keen on Gip but I think he'll come through for us. You're not the sort of person who would be friends with someone who's evil."

"You don't have to be evil not to want to help the Project."

She took her hand away and sighed. "Those who aren't with us are against us," she said in a voice that was less motherly now. "If you are not prepared to help the power of goodness, you are . . . on the other side."

"Gip doesn't do sides. He's just Gip."

A flicker of concern crossed my mother's face. "Everyone does sides," she said quietly. "You must remember that. Everyone."

I was about to ask her what she meant, but she laid a finger on my lips. "Some of us have to work," she said. "We'll talk about this later." She kissed me gently on the forehead and left me in the semi-darkness.

25 · POWER

I WAS AWOKEN later that morning by something heavy jumping on to the bed. It was Dougal. He was in one of his cat moods. Sometimes, without warning, he would seem to decide that he was not a West Highland terrier at all and go all feline on me, refusing to go for a walk in the park, curling up on my lap, even now and then trying to climb the curtains.

As he lay on my stomach, I played along with his fantasy, stroking the side of his face as if he were a big, lazy tabby. Sleepily, I told him that if the Project was producing angel-dogs like him, it must be in deep trouble. I asked him whether the Presence was trying to make a cat but somehow the recipe went wrong and the result was a Dougal-type mistake. He looked deeply into my eyes, as if to say that he was as confused by the way he carried on as I was. "You're a nutter, Doogie," I said, and he gave a little bark of embarrassment.

The door opened. I looked up to see Luke, the Surfer-Boy, standing there, a big, pearly-toothed smile on his face.

"Sorry to interrupt the conversation," he said. "I thought the dog was locked in here."

"I didn't know anyone was in the house."

Luke wandered over to my new computer and ran his hands over the keys. "Amy wanted to call by and pick up some stuff. We're taking off to Cornwall for a few days."

"Surf's up?"

I must have sounded more hostile than I intended because he looked up sharply.

"We're on the same side, Tom," he said in his most sincere voice.

"Oh yeah, of course." I smiled. "I keep forgetting that you're an angel—I can't think why."

"We're glad to have you with us."

"Who said I am?"

"I kind of assumed."

I pushed Dougal gently off my stomach and he lay on his back beside me, eyes closed, feet in the air. "I was told that the Project believed in free will."

"All is good. All will be resolved." Luke spoke these words with the unnerving inner conviction of someone who has found the way and the truth and just knows that you will be joining him soon.

"So it's my choice, right."

"Of course." He paused, then added casually, "You have a lot of power right now."

"I thought angels were meant to be the ones with the power."

"You have power over your own future." He strolled over the bed and began rubbing Dougal's stomach. "And power over your family's future."

"My family—in what way?"

He looked up at me with the perfect, Surfer-Boy smile and, at that moment, I sensed that this casual conversation was no accident. "Within the Project, we each have our own duties—our own little project, if you like," he said. "You are theirs."

"So you mean, if I fail to come through, they pay the price."

"Put it this way. There's a connection between what you decide and their future role in the Project."

"What has an angel got to worry about anyway?" I asked.

Lazily, Luke took his right hand out of his pocket. He flicked a tiny coin with his thumb, then passed it to me. "Take a look at that," he said. "We call it a kewl-disc."

"Yeah?"

"It's the key to the life of an angel—the life or the non-life."

"Are you saying angels can be killed?"

He moved his hand down Dougal's stomach and extended one of his stubby little hind legs. In the hollow between my dog's leg and his stomach, I caught sight of the tell-tale blemish. "Dougal's derm," said Luke. "Watch."

He lowered the disc on to the discolored flesh and held it there for a few seconds. Growling, Dougal opened his eyes. Then, after about five seconds, he gave a little whine, stiffened, and then relaxed as if the life was passing out of him. Luke placed a hand under his shoulder and raised him a few inches from the bed. The dog's head sagged, his tongue lolled out of his mouth.

"What have you done, you idiot?" I sat up in bed.

"The kewl-disc has closed down his circuits." Luke laid Dougal down gently on the bed. "The only way he can be re-activated is by placing the other side of the disc against his derm and that has to be done before brain death, which occurs within a few minutes."

"Do it." I looked at the unconscious form of our angel-dog. "Wake him up—now, Luke!"

"Sorry, Tom." Luke looked almost concerned. "I really didn't mean to upset you." He turned the disc over and held it against Dougal's derm. After a few seconds, the dog started breathing again.

"Don't let this worry you, Tom." Luke put his hand under Dougal's chin and seemed to be checking his eyes. "Although we each have one, kewl-discs are not used that often. I just wanted to give you a bit of guidance."

Amy appeared in the doorway. "What's going on in here?" she asked.

"Nothing much." Luke ruffled Dougal's head and winked at me. "Just three guys passing the time of day."

26 · ACTION

LATER THAT AFTERNOON, I called Gip on his
mobile. I told him that Surfer-Boy had
called by to tell me that angels could die
too.

"How's that then?" Gip seemed distracted, almost uninterested.

"They've got a kind of disc thing that
can close down an angel's circuit. Luke
killed my dog and brought him back to life
again. He said he was giving me guidance
but his message was clear—this could happen to your mum and dad."

"Your former mum and dad," he murmured. "Don't forget that they come from a
long, long way away."

"Not to me they don't." I was surprised
by how angry Gip's words made me feel.
"They're all right, my parents. They do
their best for me and I know it's not
because of some Project but because . . .
because I'm me."

"Sure." Gip paused. "Of course, it's

possible that all those feelings are part of the deal—that there's a 'Love Thomas' circuit in their inner program."

"No." I didn't like Gip talking about my family like this. Just because he was unlucky enough to have had a dad who had scrammed while he was still in nappies and a mum who seemed to be some kind of psycho, it didn't mean that all families were a fraud. "They may be aliens but they're my aliens," I said weakly.

"So now they're telling you that it's your call. You're with the angels with their freaky little derms and their magic kewl-discs or you're a free spirit, a good old human being."

I paused, taking in what Gip had just said, every word of it. "Angels are not freaky. They're good," I said eventually. "Look outside your squat and tell me truthfully that we don't need the power of angels. We can use all the help we can get, right?"

"Maybe it's me." There was a sadness in Gip's voice. "I've never been one to worry too much about anyone else, let alone the human race."

"That's not true, Gip. You've been there for me when there was nothing in it for you."

"You reckon? Well—" Gip paused, almost as if he were considering telling me something but then changed his mind. "It's your decision," he said quietly. "But don't take too long. I've got a thousand responses from adopted kids on my computer. There's definitely an angelic pattern to their stories. Come over tomorrow and we can blow this story across the world."

"You can do that whatever I decide."

"No." He spoke quickly. "If you decide that the Project is good, that you're with the angels, I promise I'll do whatever you think best. I'll wipe the messages from my computer. I'll help in any way they want."

"You're saying it's down to me."

"I'm here by accident." Gip spoke quietly. "Remember the park at the end of last term? It was you who involved me in your parents and their weird games."

"I guess that's true."

"So you get to decide which way the old Gip-and-Tom combo is going to jump. Deal?"

I thought for a moment, then said, "Deal."

I sat on my bed and stared out of the window. On the pavement across the road, a mother was making her way to the shops, pushing a baby buggy in front of her. I could hear the sound of children in the playground nearby, a distant police siren, the ghostly scream of swifts as they cut across the sky. It was a dazzling, cloudless day, perfect for the holidays, but everything I saw and heard seemed different now. Poor old humankind. It had tried and it had failed. Even on a day like this, the mark of doom was on it.

I shook my head, as if to rid myself of these thoughts. I remembered how I had been before that fateful day when Gip and I had hacked into my father's computer. Since then, every step—the holiday in California, Rendle, the realization that angels were everywhere—had seemed to persuade me that, with the Project, all is good, all will be resolved, while humankind was lost and without hope.

In fact, looking back, my whole journey might have been planned. Every step had brought me closer to the decision I was about to make. It was almost as if I had been guided here.

In my mind, I went through it all—the things that had happened, the words that had been said—and suddenly, in spite of the heat, I found that I was shivering. I saw it all, the terrifying simplicity of it, the one part of the story that I had been blind to all this time.

I understood.

I returned to the house. I went upstairs, sat for a moment in front of my computer, and switched it on.

I was back. I knew that the Presence would reach me through the computer. What I hadn't realized was that I would be transported across the world to the place where I had first seen an angel.

Within seconds of my computer coming to life, the screen turned to an unearthly purple. I heard the voices of otherworldly music all around me and the reality of my room, my computer, me, faded as I seemed to become absorbed by the screen itself.

I was in the desert. I stood before the bunker. The door opened. I was descending in the lift. I stepped out.

There before me was the landscape made of a million naked human bodies, stretching as far as the eye could see.

I stood for a moment, uncertain as to what was expected of me. Then the Presence was there. When it spoke, no sound reached my ears because the voice was within me. It was as if my own soul was speaking.

YOU HAVE TRAVELED FAR, THOMAS, AND NOW YOU HAVE ARRIVED AT YOUR DESTINATION. YOU ARE HOME. YOU ARE PART OF OUR GREAT FAMILY.

I stared ahead of me. The bodies seemed to move gently as I watched, as if they formed a great, welcoming sea of humanity.

Where am I?

THIS IS THE ANGEL FACTORY. IT IS HERE THAT THE BEINGS WHICH WILL SAVE YOUR PLANET ARE CREATED.

What do you want from me now?

YOU WILL MAKE YOUR DECISION. YOU WILL PLACE YOUR TRUST IN THE PROJECT. NO SACRIFICE WILL BE REQUIRED OF YOU. YOU WILL KNOW WHAT TO DO.

I will know.

IT IS AN HONORABLE THING THAT YOU ARE DOING, THOMAS.

The music returned. I looked down and the angels that were there smiled their welcome. Although they were naked, I was free of any kind of embarrassment. I saw them as they were, as kind and innocent as babies. As I looked, I saw that, within a few strides of where I was standing, there was a space among the bodies and I knew that it was for me if I joined the Project. One last task awaited me back on Earth.

YOU WILL MAKE YOUR DECISION.

I WILL MAKE MY DECISION.

ALL IS GOOD. ALL WILL BE RESOLVED.

I turned and walked towards the bright, unearthly light of the lift. The door closed behind me and I felt a great feeling of loneliness and fear. The motion stopped and sunlight flooded the lift.

I shook my head, placed my thumb and forefinger over my eyes. The music faded.

I looked about me. I was back in my room. There on the screen before me was a single word against a deep purple background.

DECIDE.

I walked to my parents' bedroom. An hour or so remained before their return from work. I searched, methodically and without panic. And there, in my mother's jewelry box, I found what I was looking for.

I called Gip and told him that I knew what I had to do. We agreed to meet at the squat the following day. It was time for action.

27 · SEND

IT WAS SWELTERING the next day when I
headed east. As I waited in a queue at the
bus stop, a guy in a suit was talking to his
office on a cell phone, giving it full volume
for the benefit of the rest of us. From what
he said, I gathered that parts of Central
London were closed. There was, as he put
it, "traffic chaos big-time."

Chaos? Closed streets? My first thought
was that some kind of Project-related
weirdness was coming down but then the
mobile-shouter started complaining about
politicians messing everything up, as usual.
Apparently, there was a conference taking
place in the center of the city. Big-shot
leaders, including the American President,
had flown in from all over the world. There
were worries about demonstrations and the
rest of us, including Big-Mouth on his
mobile, were being made to suffer.

I reached the house an hour late but
Gip seemed not to have noticed. He looked

pale and ghost-like, as if he had been living off air and chewing-gum for the past few days. In the old days, when we met, we would slip into an easy kind of conversation, sometimes picking up where we left off hours or even days before. Now he glanced at me with a wary, dark-eyed look, said, "Hey, Tom," and turned into the house. Suddenly, for Gip, I represented all the trouble in his troubled life.

We went to his room. Because the window had to remain closed to keep out the noise and fumes of motorway traffic, it was steaming hot.

"It's like a sauna in here," I said.

"Yeah?" Gip flapped his big old denim shirt under which he was wearing his usual gray T-shirt. "Doesn't bother me."

I found a shady corner and sat on the floor. "I used my computer last night," I said.

He frowned and sat down slowly on the stool in front of his laptop. "I thought that was meant to be a dodgy, brainwashing thing."

"It is. I was taken back to Seraph."

Gip gave a sharp, humorless laugh. "They've got an airplane in there too?"

"I don't know how it's done. But I was there and it felt real. They call it the Angel Factory."

"An underground wonderworld—the same as before?"

"Sort of. Only this time, I had a guide. The Presence."

Gip glanced out of the window. He was acting casual but I wasn't taken in. "And what did old Presence have to say?" he asked.

"He told me the moment to decide had come. I would be with the Project. I was part of the family."

"Doesn't sound like much of a choice to me."

"The Presence told me what I should do but, even as it spoke, I knew one thing for sure. I am human, not an angel.

That means that I'm free to choose. It was why I risked turning on the computer. I needed to go through that. It gave me a sort of strength."

"Are you saying no to the Project?" Gip asked softly.

"I'm saying no to the Project."

Gip looked away. He gazed out of the window for a few seconds. The great traffic disaster had reached the motorway outside. A haze of smog and heat hung over the queues of cars and lorries. It was as if, at that moment, the whole world had stopped and was being baked under a pitiless sun.

A bead of sweat ran down the side of his face. He turned back to me and said in a voice that was almost a whisper, "Are you sure about this?"

I stood up and walked over to where he sat. "I'm sure. Turn on the computer." I looked down on his damp and matted hair. "And take off that stupid shirt, will you?" I said. "It's making me sweat just looking at you."

He wriggled out of the shirt, chucked it on the floor and switched on the laptop. When he went on-line, the message in the top left-hand corner read, You have 2,157 messages.

"Kids of the world unite," I said.

"Right," muttered Gip.

"So what we do is tell these people—every one of them—the facts about the Project. We say we're setting up a network for kids who are being recruited into it."

Gip opened up a blank e-mail. He typed in the words "AN IMPORTANT MESSAGE."

I began to dictate.

Here is some information of the greatest importance for you. There is an extraterrestrial force on earth. It is infiltrating mankind with human-like creatures it describes as "angels." Although its motives are said to be friendly, you should know that many children who have been adopted have been taken into families of angels. Your reply to my earlier message suggests that you may be one of them.

This means that each of you has a choice. You can either support what angels call the Project by remaining silent and agreeing to do what your adoptive parents tell you. Or you can resist.

I have decided to resist. I am offering a support group for those like me. I am not sure what our next step should be—only that, together, we are strong.

Remember, you may be adopted for all the usual, human reasons—if so, this message is not for you. But, if you know that you are among angels, then you need know only this.

You are not alone.
Signed
Thomas Wisdom

Gip sat back. "Seems kind of whacko," he said.

"Whacko, but true."

He looked over his shoulder at me, his hair falling to one side. "Once it's gone, there's no turning back," he said.

"I know that."

"The thing is—" Gip turned on his stool and faced me. He seemed smaller and more vulnerable than he had ever been before. "We can't send the messages out right now. We have to batch them."

"Batch?"

"There are rules about flaming on the Internet—that's sending out an e-mail to thousands of people. So, if we tried to send all the e-mails together, the server would close me down. Only ten or fifteen would make it. I'll batch them in fifties tonight." He shrugged his narrow shoulders. "It's a drag but at least we'll get through."

"I'll stay. We could do it together now."

"No." Gip's eyes held mine with an odd defiance. "I'll do it later."

"Why wait?"

"What's your problem? You think I'm bottling out, is that it?"

"Of course I don't." There was a hint of pleading in my voice. "Come on, Gip. How long would it take?"

I smiled at him, willing him with all my heart to be the Gip that I knew, that I understood, but he shook his head.

"I don't think so," he said. "The fact is, people around here are getting kind of iffy about your hanging out in the house. They've decided you're a security risk."

"They don't even know me."

"You look straight. You turn up in the middle of the night. If you had lived the kind of lives they lead, you'd understand."

"We've been in this together from the start. Now we've got—"

"What is this?" He leaned forward and for a moment I thought he was going to hit me. "Don't you trust me? After everything we've been through?"

For a full ten seconds we stared at each other. "The old Gip-and-Tom combo," I said quietly. "Of course I trust you."

Gip smiled with relief. "It'll be done by midnight."

I nodded in the direction of the laptop. "Hadn't you better save our message?"

He turned back to the screen and, as he crouched over the keyboard, the hair on his shoulders parted and I saw what I needed to see.

I got up and crossed the room. Standing behind him, I reached into my pocket and took out the kewl-disc. It radiated warmth into my fingers.

On the screen were the words "SEND" and "SAVE."

Gip was moving the cursor. With an unspoken prayer, I laid the disc gently on Gip, on his shoulder, on his derm. He froze for a few seconds. I held firm. Then he slumped forward, lifeless, and toppled sideways on to the floor.

I knelt over him, tears in my eyes. I felt his neck for a pulse. There was nothing.

I put the disc back into my pocket. I sat in front of the computer and double-clicked on "SAVE." For a few seconds, the screen seemed to freeze before a message appeared, reading, E-mail saved. I closed down the laptop, put it in its bag and, hooking it over my shoulder, walked to the door.

With one last look at the body of my best friend, I left the room and closed the door behind me. I walked down the stairs and let myself out of the house. The suffocatingly warm air hit me, startled me into life. Head down, I walked away quickly towards the bus stop.

28 · TRUTH

GIP WAS AN ANGEL.

The evidence had been there all the time, staring me in the face. His hideout, his computer, his mobile phone, the mysterious way that cash never seemed to be a problem for him. All could be explained by one terrifying truth.

Gip was an angel.

It was the unavoidable answer to questions that I had tried so hard to ignore. How had Dover known about my suspicions about Rendle's nurse when I had only talked to Gip after he had phoned the headteacher? What had he meant, after the teacher's death, that I "knew nothing about anything"? How was it that Dover had casually let slip to him the details of where my real mother could be found? Why was he so unsurprised by the effect my computer had on me?

Gip was an angel.

At first, I couldn't believe it. I wouldn't

believe it. But then, yesterday, the proof was there. He had let slip the words "that kewl-disc thing." The only problem was that I had said nothing about its name among angels— I had only mentioned that it was a disc.

Gip was an angel.

I had remembered Rendle, the subtle warnings I had been given by my mother, by Amy. "Those who aren't with us are against us." "The Project comes first." I understood that, in the deadly game of saving humanity from itself, a life here or there was expendable. Like Rendle, I knew too much. When Gip refused to send the message to the world, he left me no alternative.

Gip was an angel.

It was me or him. A world fit for humans or one run by the Project. I had no choice.

29 · KEY

FOR A WHILE I WALKED without thinking, holding the laptop against me, gazing ahead with unseeing eyes. Gip was my past, my present. Whatever had happened in my life, he had been there, unfazed by anything, my friend. I had become used to comparing my little misadventures with the bad things that had happened to him. If Gip could come through, I had believed, anyone could.

In my mind, I heard his voice. I tried to imagine a future without him. I saw my hand, pressed against his neck. I stopped walking, closed my eyes and the tears spilled over and ran down my cheeks.

I sat on a low wall, head down. Footsteps hurried by—in this part of town, people avoid trouble as if it's an infectious disease.

Gip was an angel, a dead angel. I thought back to the moment yesterday when Luke had shown me how the kewldisc cut out the circuit of life in Dougal. He had brought Dougal back to life with the reverse side of the coin but he had said he had to act quickly.

I looked around. Across the road, which was clogged with traffic, there was a telephone box. I rang my father's work number.

"Thomas." He sounded eerily normal. "What a nice surprise."

"Gip." I managed the word with difficulty. "He's at 34 Chesterton Close."

"You've spoken to him? He's agreed?"

"Don't lie!" It was a bellow of agony. "You know what he is. Get there now. Please, save his life, Dad!"

I hung up.

As I stepped out into the blazing sun, my first instinct, without thinking, was to head back to the flat, to bring Gip round if it wasn't too late, to ask him what we should do next. But now I was on my own. Dead or alive, Gip was with the angels, on the other side. The laptop weighed heavy on my shoulder. In the electric circuits of that gray plastic box was a network of contacts with children about to be recruited for the Project. I understood why Gip had wanted to delay sending out the fateful e-mail that would blow the Project wide open, but why had he taken me to that point? Was he setting me up for some kind of sinister test or had he wanted to rebel against his angelic masters by helping me expose what they were doing? If so, why did he lose his nerve at that crucial last moment?

I thought back to how he looked at the flat. The Gip I had once known—so strong, so true to himself—was no longer there. He was a soul in torment, forced to act against his inner nature. But which was the true Gip—my friend or the servant of the angels? Maybe I would never know.

I remembered the laptop. It had been tempting to

dispatch the e-mails at the flat, to press "SEND" and leave the computer there, but I had sensed that Gip had been right about the batching business. At some point, that message to the 2,157 children who were waiting for it would have to be sent out systematically, but not now. I had to find somewhere to leave the laptop where no angel could find it.

At that moment, I noticed a bus edging towards me in the heavy traffic. The sign on the front read, Victoria Station. Travelers. Luggage. It was worth a try.

The doors drew back and I stepped on.

It took me almost two hours to get there. The traffic moved like sludge. Looking out the window, I noticed newspaper headlines—*PRESIDENT FOXX JETS IN*, they read, as if to remind me why, on this of all days, moving around town was almost impossible.

When I reached the station, I followed the signs to the Left-Luggage Office. At first, when I saw the wall of metal lockers, it seemed to me that there were none to spare but, as I stood in front of them, wondering what to do next, an American student type arrived, pulled a key out of his pocket, opened a locker and removed his suitcase.

I stepped forward, put the laptop into the locker, found a coin, and locked it.

Slowly, I walked through the milling crowds at the station, the small key held tightly in the palm of my hand. How many of these commuters were angels? Who could I trust with the key? I thought of Manny, who had seemed human enough, but then, as I had discovered, angels came in all shapes and sizes. Besides, I had no idea where to find him.

I slipped the key into my pocket and, as I did so, my fingers touched a card. I took it out and read the words, "The Great Miraculo (and his lovely assistant Maria Procchutti)

Comedy and Magic!" In my mind, I heard the voice of Karen, my real mother. "If you're ever in trouble . . . I'd like to make it up to you somehow."

There was a newsagent nearby. I bought some writing paper, a brown envelope, a ballpoint pen, and a stamp. Ignoring the stares of passers-by, I sat on the tarmac and, leaning against a wall, began to write a letter to the one person I knew who could not be an angel—the woman who had brought me into the world.

It was not a long letter and I knew that, when she read my hurried words, Karen Garnham would almost certainly conclude that I was some kind of nutter, but it was a risk I had to take.

I slipped the key into the envelope with the letter and posted it. Then, on an impulse, I walked to a phone-booth, took out the card and dialed the number of the mobile that was on it. She picked up on the third ring.

I hesitated, then spoke. "Er, Karen, it's Thomas Wisdom."

"Who?"

"Your son."

She laughed and I knew that she was pleased to hear my voice. "Oh hello, Thomas, love," she said.

"I can't talk for long. I just wanted to say that I've sent you a letter with a key. If anything happens to me, read the letter. It'll tell you where a computer is. You've got to send out an e-mail. I've explained it all."

I heard the voice of the Great Miraculo muttering in the background. "Listen, love." Karen sounded distracted. "It's not a good moment for a joke. We're on our way to an audition."

"This is not a joke. If I ever meant anything to you, please take it seriously."

"But I don't know anything about computers and all that."

"It's not difficult. Get someone to help you."

"Honestly, it's a bit of a—"

"Please. Remember what you said to me—about making it all up to me."

I heard that smoky chuckle of hers. "Me and my big mouth." She paused, as if she were thinking it over. "All right then."

"D'you promise?"

"Of course I promise," she said. "You're my son, aren't you?"

I thanked her and hung up.

It was time to go home.

30 · VIP

THEY WERE WAITING FOR ME. I knew they would be.

At the end of the street were two police motorbikes. Their riders stood chatting to one another, their helmets on the seats of the bikes. As I walked past, they glanced at me and one of them picked up the intercom from the side of his machine and muttered something into the mouthpiece.

A big black limo was outside the front door. As I approached, I recognized the man sitting at the driver's seat. It was Luke, wearing a dark suit. Surfer-Boy had gone straight. I raised a hand in greeting as I walked past. He stared back at me with a wary, guarded look and for the first time I realized that, to those involved in the Project, I now represented danger, the unpredictable.

As I let myself in, I heard my mother's voice. "Here he is," she said, and there was a warmth and relief in her voice that made the breath catch in my throat.

She came out of the kitchen, smiling. She held me in her arms for a moment. "Oh, Thomas," she murmured. My father stood at the sitting-room door. He looked as if he hadn't slept for a week. "Are you all right, old boy?" he asked.

"Did they get to Gip?"

"We haven't been told." My father gazed at me for a moment. "Why did you do it?" he asked quietly.

I shook my head. I was searching for words to explain what I had done when the voice of Cy Gabriel could be heard from the sitting-room. "We're on our way," he was saying. "We'll be there in fifteen."

He emerged from the room, slipping his mobile phone into his jacket pocket.

"Ready to roll, Wisdoms?" There was a new, boss-like coldness in his voice.

Mum looked at me. "Pop upstairs and wash your face," she said. "You look a mess."

"What's happening?" I asked.

Dad seemed about to answer but Cy cut in. "You'll find out, Thomas. Let's move it, OK?"

When I came back downstairs, the three of them were standing in silence. Cy and Dad made their way out of the front door. Mum put her arm around me and we followed.

The police motorbikes were in front of the car, their lights flashing. Cy stepped into the front seat. I sat between my parents in the back.

Suddenly we were in some kind of VIP motorcade. With the help of the robocops out front, we cut across traffic, through red lights, made our way out of London in the fast lane of the motorway.

I looked out of the darkened window but the world outside suddenly seemed far away, as if it belonged to a different planet. I had done something which had taken me beyond humanity and placed me, full of shame and self-hatred, among the angels. I had killed my best friend.

I turned to my mother. "What about Gip?" I said. "I must know what's happened to him."

She squeezed my hand. "All is good," she murmured. "All will be resolved."

After about ten minutes, we left the main road, heading towards some kind of air force base guarded by high-security wire. As we approached the gates, a barrier rose and we swept through without even slowing down.

We passed some buildings then took a sharp turn towards the open expanse of a runway.

"Where are we going?" I asked, alarmed now. "What's going on?"

No one answered. Ahead of us, on the runway, I saw a sleek private jet. "I haven't got my passport," I said.

I moved closer to my mother. "I don't want to be taken to the Angel Factory," I said. "Don't let them, Mum, please."

The limo drew up beside the long metal steps leading up to the plane. Cy, my mother, and my father got out of the car. I followed. A man in a trim dark suit was waiting at the top of the steps.

"We'll see you in a moment, Thomas," said Cy Gabriel.

I looked up the steps. "You're not coming?"

My mother smiled. "It's OK," she said. "We'll be here." She kissed me lightly on the cheek. "Remember your manners."

Slowly, I walked up the steps. At the top, the man smiled oddly. "Just a quick search now, son," he said in an American accent.

I held out my arms. He padded around my body for a while.

"Still got the disc?" he asked.

I had forgotten about that. I reached into my back pocket and handed the kewl-disc to him. "Follow me, please," he said, turning into the darkness of the plane.

He knocked on a door. A sing-song voice called out "Ya" from inside. The door opened into an office. Behind a big desk, wearing shirt-sleeves and smiling broadly, was the most powerful man in the world.

"So. Welcome, Thomas Wisdom," said the president of the United States.

31 · HUMAN

MY FIRST THOUGHT was that, through some angelic strangeness, I had been absorbed into a monitor screen once more, that all this—the journey, the plane, President Foxx—was not real but one of the living dreams that seem to be part of the Project. At the throw of a switch I would be back in my room, blinking in front of my computer.

But there was nothing virtual about President Jim Foxx. He stepped forward and, in one movement, grasped my right hand in that great paw of his while holding my left forearm. "At last we meet," he said, gazing at me with this big smile, as if his life had been empty until I walked into his plane. And, weirdly, I felt happy too at that moment—proud to be in the presence of this big, swaggering, blond-haired cowboy of a man.

He was gazing at me as if expecting some kind of response.

"Hi." The word emerged from the back

of my throat. It sounded like the distant cry of a seagull.

The President of the United States looked me straight in the eye as if what I had just said was the wisest thing he had ever heard. Reluctantly he let go of my hand. "Coke? Beer?" He walked over to a cocktail cabinet in the corner.

"Coke, please," I croaked.

He opened the cabinet and took out two cans. He gave me one, opened a can of beer for himself, then eased his big frame into the chair behind the desk. Taking a long, thirsty swig at the beer, he said, "Now don't you go telling the press that the President drinks on the job." He smiled at me as if we were best friends. "I got enough problems already."

"I don't understand." I spoke quietly. "What are you—? I mean, what am I doing here?"

The President chuckled, as if at the sheer craziness of the idea that good old Jim Foxx had ended up in Air Force One. "I didn't fly in to see Thomas Wisdom, if that's what you're thinking. There was a conference and my people mentioned that you and I might have a word about one or two problems we share." He picked up a sheet of typed paper that was lying on his desk and read it for a moment. "We need to talk, Thomas," he said, more serious now. "Man to man."

"Man to angel."

President Foxx smiled. "You ain't telling me you're surprised that the President is part of the Project?"

"Kind of."

"You seem to be in the habit of underestimating us."

I sat in silence. I suppose I should have felt alarmed at this point, maybe even afraid, but somehow the President exuded a warmth, almost a sense of companionship, that made me feel as if we were both in this together, that there was no problem in the world that could not be solved by a couple of guys, swigging their drinks and talking it over.

"Here's the thing," he said eventually. "You have a kinda privileged position in what we call the Project. You're the future, Thomas—the first generation of true humans that can change the course of history."

He looked at me significantly.

"Great," I said.

"See." He shifted his position as if he were about to tell a long story. "Our job is not to save humanity, but to empower it. You guys have to choose life yourselves. We're here to present the options. Then it's up to you."

I knew what I was meant to be doing. The President of the United States was talking to me about the future of the planet. My duty was to sit in respectful silence and listen. But the more this big, confident man treated me like his greatest buddy in the world, the less I was able to shift the image of my real friend, lying lifelessly on the floor of his room.

Mistaking my silence for nervousness, the President was about to start talking again, but it was me who spoke first.

"What happened to Gip?" I asked.

"Gip?" The President's eyes flickered uncertainly over the paper before him.

"Gary Sanchez," I said.

"Ah, Gary." The President sat back in his chair. "You mean the guy you killed."

"I thought angels were de-activated."

"Yeah, right, whatever. Gary's fine."

I was overcome by a great surge of relief. "He's not dead?"

"He's not dead—at least not in the important, Project sense of the word." The President smiled broadly like some dodgy preacher bringing news of the Promised Land. "When an angel is de-activated on Earth, his essence returns home. Believe me, Tom." He gazed at me with damp-eyed sincerity. "Your friend Gip is in a far better place."

I closed my eyes for a moment. I knew then that I hated the Project. The last doubt in my mind as to what I had to do had disappeared.

"You all right, Tom?"

"I'm fine," I said quietly. "You were telling me how it is down to me to decide my future."

"That's right. We prepared the ground. With our help, you discovered the truth about your adoption. You visited the Angel Factory. The Presence entered your life. You learned about the Project and its importance for mankind."

"All that was set up."

"We merely laid the path. You walked it."

"And Mr. Rendle? Was he part of the path?"

The President gave an easy, win-some-lose-some shrug. "Life's full of tough choices, Thomas. It was important for you to see that the Project is not just a bowl of candies. Sacrifices have to be made for the greater good."

"Are you saying that Mr. Rendle had to die just so that I understood how serious the Project was?"

"There was more to it than that. He knew stuff. Our people weren't happy about the way he had cracked our code. He might just have persuaded you to download more files from your dad's computer. It was all getting kinda messy."

"So you tidied up."

"That's right." The President spoke with a hint of impatience in his voice. "They say he wasn't the greatest teacher anyway."

"If everything was arranged for me, where did the choice come in?"

"OK." The President placed his big hands behind his head. "So you are guided by angels—Cy, your parents, your friend Gip."

"But Gip was always on my side."

"Precisely. His function was to offer you an alternative to joining the Project—the path of rebellion. To be a devil's advocate. We needed to see if an average guy like Thomas Wisdom—bright, kind, normal—would understand what we were doing. We would offer you everything but Gip would be there to tempt you with the other, less responsible way. He would show you how the Project sometimes came at a high human cost with the whole Rendle thing. He would take you to your real mother. He would even offer you the chance to destroy our work. Then it would be a true choice for you. We have one or two similar experiments going on in different parts of the world. Yours went critical before the rest."

"Except, when Gip contacted all those adopted kids across the world and I dictated that letter, that was where my freedom came to an end."

"We may be good, but we're not stupid. Gip was under instructions to delay sending your letter out, so that we could talk to you, show you the implications of what you were doing."

I thought of what had happened to Rendle. "Talk to me?"

"We were convinced you'd see sense. Until then you'd been a perfect subject."

"That's the thing about us humans," I said sharply. "Just when you think you understand us, we go and do the unpredictable thing."

"Yeah." The President frowned. "We're going to have to do something about that."

"I made a choice, didn't I? For the first time I left that precious path of yours. I found out Gip was an angel and I closed his circuits with my mother's kewl-disc."

For the first time, the President looked displeased. "You messed up our plans big-time."

"Sorry about that, Mr. President." I felt sad, thinking of Gip and how our friendship had been part of the Project.

"But, hey, let's be positive, Tom." The President leaned forward and rested his head on his big hands. "We know it's not too late. Our information is that there are no signs of inappropriate activity from our targeted children around the world. That e-mail hasn't been sent."

I said nothing.

"In which case—" He winked at me as if we were involved in some kind of private game. "There's absolutely no reason why we can't still do business."

"What kind of business?"

"All you need to do is let us know where to find the computer, agree to tell no one anything about this, and let us get back on track with the Project."

"What about the other kids around the world you've been taking down the path?"

"They're no longer your problem, Tom. You're free of all that."

There was silence in Air Force One. Through one of the small, circular windows, I could see two soldiers, both with serious-looking guns slung over the shoulders, chatting to one another.

"So." The President smiled. "Here's what we can do. You and I—together, now—can reach an agreement. You give us what we need and life goes back to normal. As far as you're concerned, none of this will have happened."

"Except my math teacher is dead, I've discovered that my parents come from outer space, and I've lost my best friend."

"Stuff happens, Tom. You'll learn that one day." He glanced at his watch and stood up. "So if you'd like to tell Cy Gabriel where to get hold of the computer, we can draw a line under the whole story."

He walked around to my side of the desk and stood over me, his hands sunk in his trouser pockets. "It's decision time, Tom," he said with quiet menace.

Suddenly, I felt small and alone. One by one, the people I loved or depended on had been revealed as angels. Now the President of the United States was giving me one, simple instruction. Yes. It was all I had to say in order to be given back my family, my life, for me to be free, for the events of the past weeks to start fading like a nightmare in the morning sun.

"Do yourself a favor, kid," said the President, jangling some loose change in his pocket.

I looked out of the window at the countryside beyond the tarmac of the airport. Out there, all over the world, men and women and children were going about their daily business. They were laughing and crying and loving and hurting and doing all the good and bad things, making all the right and wrong choices, that made them human. I saw Rendle crouched in front of his mum. I heard Manny's loud, innocent laugh in the darkness of the theater. I remembered my own, my real mother holding me in her arms. "You're a good kid," she had said.

Then I thought of the Presence, the Project, Cy Gabriel, and the President of the United States and the clean, trouble-free future they promised for us all.

"Well?" The President laid a hand on my shoulder.

I took a deep breath and tried to speak but my mouth was dry and all I could manage was a despairing croak. I swallowed, cleared my throat, closed my eyes—and said it loud and clear.

"No."

The President looked down at me, as if unable to believe what he had just heard. "What was that, Thomas?" he said.

"No."

He took his hand off my shoulder. "You're telling me you don't want to save humanity from self-destruction?"

"No." Feeling stronger now, I took a swig from my can of Coke. When I spoke again, my voice was flat and even, as if a machine were talking. I told him that it was all too late. The full story had been told to a human that no angel had reached. If anything happened to me, the computer would be found and the e-mail would be sent out to adopted children all over the world. I said that there was nothing anybody could do about this. "I am not going to change my mind," I said. "I've seen enough of the Project to know that, however noble its aims, all is not good."

The President turned his back on me and gazed down at the security guards outside.

"And all will not be resolved," I said. "Further down the line, there will be loads of people who'll feel like me. In the end, like it or not, you'd have to save us by force."

The President's shoulders gave a sort of shrug in reply.

"We might be a mess," I said. "But that's the way we like it. That's the way we are."

He turned and slumped back into his chair, looking tired and pale now, as if, at the throw of a switch, the warmth and color that had glowed from him moments ago had been closed down.

"Who the hell d'you think you are?" He spoke wearily. "Some geeky little kid who can throw all our plans for a loop because he can't see the big picture, because he's so—" An expression of disgust crossed his face "so human."

"That sounds about right," I said.

"Does it occur to you that, if the Project is deactivated, little Thomas Wisdom will be in the world without his parents, without his sister? You're not just letting me and the whole Project down, you're betraying your own family."

I thought for a moment of my life and how good it had been. I saw us in the garden, the sun shining, Dougal on the lawn engaged in a fight to the death with an old tennis ball. "I think I'm doing what they would want me to do," I said.

"They're angels, Tom."

"I know what they are."

He sighed wearily. "Let's go through this once more. Perhaps I can help you in some other areas—as a gesture of good faith."

"Mr. President, you're wasting your time."

"You don't know what you're turning down yet. I can make your life pretty good. Hey, how about making sure that your parents never have to work again?"

"I mean it," I said.

He glared at me for a moment, as if the sheer force of his will could make me change my mind, but I held his gaze. He swore quietly to himself, then pressed the button on his desk. The door behind me opened.

"I'll see Gabriel," he told the security guard as he scribbled something on the typed piece of paper on his desk. After a moment, he glanced up and seemed irritable that I was still in his presence. "Scram, kid," he said coldly.

"Thank you, Mr. President," I said.

I walked to the door.

"Go back to your family and don't leave home until we tell you," said the President.

The guard closed the door behind me. I made my way to the entrance of Air Force One and stepped out into the dazzling sun. My parents and Cy Gabriel were standing on the tarmac like a reception party.

I stood at the top of the steps, feeling suddenly tired, alone and frightened. I shook my head slowly and they understood. As I walked down, I noticed that the faces of my father and Cy Gabriel were not so much angry as blank and impassive. Only my mother smiled. She held out both arms as I approached and held me close.

The guard called Cy and my father over to him and they spoke for a few seconds. Cy climbed the steps for his meeting with the President.

Dad returned to us. He stood in front of me, hands in his pockets, an empty, desolate look on his face and I sensed that he was working on that stern-father act that he has never quite mastered. He shook his head slowly. "Another fine mess you've got us into," he said.

He walked on to the car where Luke was sitting in the driving-seat.

"Home," he said.

32 · HOPE

MAYBE, ALL OVER THE WORLD, there were people who were making the same decision as I had made, or were making the opposite decision, or had closed their eyes to the existence of angels altogether and were continuing their lives as if nothing had happened.

Right now, I didn't care. The future of Planet Earth was no longer what I was thinking about. As we drove back into town at a normal speed, unaccompanied by robocops on motorbikes, what was on my mind was the future of me.

I had told the President of the United States, the most powerful person—the most powerful angel—in the world, that I would be no part of the Project. He knew that I had betrayed it to humans.

What next? They had the power to destroy any little anti-angel movement. The President had rabbited on about my importance to their plans. Now that I stood in the way of the Project, what would happen to me? Some unfortunate little accident around the home, at school, on the street? Who could I trust? My mother's arm was around me now but it occurred to me that she might be comforting me or, on the other hand, restraining me from any crazy idea of escape. I was surrounded by angels. It would take one word for the little pocket of resistance that was Thomas Wisdom to be rubbed out.

We traveled home in silence. Luke dropped us off at the house and then swept away in his big black limousine. When we let ourselves in, Amy and Dougal greeted us in the hall. By the expression on my sister's face, I could tell that she had heard the news.

Muttering that I was tired, I went to my room and closed the door. In a moment of curiosity, I switched on the computer in the corner. It was dead, as if its circuits too had been closed down. I lay on my bed and closed my eyes.

It must have been several minutes later when I heard a soft knock on my door. Amy put her head round the door. "Got a moment?" she asked.

"Sure," I said.

She sat on the bed and gave me the that's-torn-it smile I knew so well. "Always the awkward one, eh, bro?" she murmured.

"I did what was right."

"Yeah. You did."

"So where do you stand on all this?"

"It doesn't matter what I think."

I sat up and asked the question that had been on my mind all day. "Could you have saved Gip?"

My sister looked out of the window for a moment. "No," she said. "We passed the information over. Apparently it was too late."

"They let him die."

Amy said nothing.

"And they are you," I said.

"Listen." Amy put an arm around my shoulders. "Mum's downstairs, crying. Dad's sitting like a stunned zombie in the kitchen. All I want to do is talk to my little brother. Even Dougal seems a bit more freaked than usual. D'you really have to ask? We love you. In fact—" she frowned as if she were surprised by what she was thinking. "We probably love you even more now than we did before. Our little Thomas, who told the President of the United States to get lost. Understand?"

I understood. "Thanks," I said.

And with that, weirdly, we returned to a sort of family routine. Mum cooked the meals I liked. We talked about the family and school and how I would miss Gip as if there was no great Project-shaped cloud hanging over the future of the Wisdom family. Only when one of the family went out, making sure that the other two stayed with me, was I reminded with a thump of anxiety in the solar plexus that I was under house arrest.

One day, two days, three. It is a strange fact that, locked away with my family, awaiting word of our fate, I felt closer to them than I had ever been. Before I had known that they came from another planet, I had been aware of a gulf of misunderstanding between us. Now I knew everything about the distance between us, there were no secrets, and we could all be ourselves, free of the secrets and lies of the past. Mum and Dad and Amy no longer went to work but spent their time with me.

Talking. Laughing. And waiting.

On the evening of the third day, Cy Gabriel appeared at our door without warning. He had the pale, crumpled look of a man who has done too much talking and not enough sleeping.

"Cy." When Dad uttered that word, it was as if an electric shock ran through the house. I had been in the kitchen with my mother, who moved closer to me, putting an arm around my shoulders as if that could protect me. When we followed Dad and Cy into the sitting-room, Amy was there, with Dougal.

I sat on the sofa between my mother and my father. Dougal looked up at me, as if he could sense that this was not a normal family gathering. I patted my lap and he jumped up.

Standing in the center of the room, Cy glanced at me, briefly and without affection.

My father noticed his look. "You say what you have to say to us all." He smiled coldly at his boss. "The four of us are in this together."

"Very touching." Cy smiled wearily and lowered himself into a chair like an old man. "But I guess you're right. The time for secrets is past."

He sat back and, as if reciting from a speech learned by heart, he told us our fate.

"Over the past few days, consultation has taken place over the future of the Project. This is our formal resolution. Some years ago, it was decided that a course of beneficent intervention was the best and most advisable way to prevent this planet from following a course of self-destruction. Angels were constructed in the form of humankind. Thanks to our co-operative network and intelligence assistance from the Presence, they reached positions of influence throughout the globe. Two years ago, the first phase of the Project was successfully completed with the election of James Foxx as President of the United States."

"Cut to the chase, Cy," Dad murmured.

"We are a force of peace. We represent goodness. It was always intended that we should enable humankind to save itself. Its future was, and is, in its children. The second phase of the Project would involve the recruitment of those who had been adopted nine, ten or eleven years ago by certain designated angels. They were guided towards the Project. They were introduced to its aims. They communicated with the Presence. Then they were asked to decide— as important a moment in our Project as the election of the President. The facts were laid before them. The path of goodness stretched into the future. All that was required of them was their co-operation with the force of angels."

Cy directed his gaze at me. "We now see that we underestimated the human desire for autonomy—what they like to call 'freedom.' During the second phase, a choice was made. We believe it was the wrong choice. The possibility of further persuasion, of selective elimination of problem areas, has been considered."

My mother moved closer to me and placed her hand on mine.

"We do not by nature abandon major projects of improvement before they are satisfactorily completed," Cy continued. "But, on this occasion, we will. The Project is over. The future of humankind will be left to humankind to resolve without our assistance. Within twelve hours, President Foxx will announce that he will not be seeking re-election for a second term."

"What about us?" Amy's voice was a whisper.

"Angels shall report to their factories for their annual reconfiguration in the normal manner but, on this occasion, a final circuit shall be installed in which the human genome, with all its faults and frailties, will be reproduced.

This will mean that angels will live as healthily or unhealthily, as happily or sadly, or as long or as short as any normal being. The randomness of life on Earth has been perfectly replicated. During their lives, angels will be part of humankind. When their circuit is closed—when they die, in human terms—they shall return to the Presence to be at peace. Within twelve months of this announcement, all traces of our involvement with humankind will have vanished."

As if he had suddenly realized what was being said affected him, Dougal looked up from my lap. "What about the animals?" I asked.

"The animals." Cy hesitated. "Angels will be provided with kewl-circuits to adapt them to a lifespan appropriate to Earth-life."

He turned to me. "Thomas, you are required to retrieve the computer from the hiding-place you chose for it. Its first contact with an electrical current will destroy the hard disk. Bring it home. Plug it in. Switch it on. It will then be good only for scrap."

I nodded my agreement.

He smiled coldly at me, then continued. "It is to be regretted that this great Project, perhaps one of the most ambitious policies in the history of the universe, has had to be terminated prematurely. Yet we are obliged to recognize that the desire of humankind for freedom, its need to decide its own fate for itself, has encouraged us. The future of the Earth, we always believed, rested in its children and its children have given us hope."

Cy Gabriel stood up. "On behalf of the Presence and the many guides and operatives behind our great Project, I bestow upon humankind our good wishes and prayers for the future."

He shook our hands, first Amy's, then my parents', finally—after a moment's hesitation—mine. "Good luck, Thomas," he said. "You're on your own now."

I smiled. "I guess."

We followed him from the room, let him out the front door. He walked away without a backward glance.

For a moment, after he was gone, the four of us stood wordlessly in the hall. Uneasy at this strange and unusual silence, Dougal looked up at us and barked.

"He needs a walk," my mother murmured.

"Life goes on," said Dad.

I picked up the key from the hall table, Dougal's lead from the hook behind the door.

"Yeah." I smiled and my smile took in all of them, all of my family. "Life goes on."

We were free. I was free. My family of angels was just the Wisdom family, now and for the future. After their next visit to the Angel Factory, Mum, Dad, and Amy would be on their own. Their lives would be as uncontrolled, mysterious, and surprising as any human's. It was going to take some getting used to but, through it all, we would be equal at last. That sense of not quite belonging to one another which first caused me to talk to Gip and set the events of the summer in motion was fading with every second.

Of course, life would never be quite the same. Mum and Dad would have to find a new job. Amy's relationship with Luke, the surfing chauffeur, would change.

I would be without Gip Sanchez. Every time I thought of him, I saw him lying at my feet, my right hand glowing with the kewl-disc, I felt a lurch of panic in my gut. No more chats on the phone, jokes, and meetings in the park. Right now, life seemed empty without him.

In kind of a daze, we each went about our business that

evening, chatting occasionally about what Cy Gabriel had said.

Later, I went upstairs and took out the card that was still in my trouser pocket. There was one more call to make. I walked to my parents' bedroom, closed the door, sat on their bed and dialed the number.

"Karen, it's Thomas."

"Hi, Thomas. What's cookin'?" The voice sounded slightly slurred.

"Did you get my letter and the key?"

"I did." She seemed uncertain as to what exactly she should say. "You are all right, aren't you, love? Your dad was a bit doolally sometimes. Maybe you should see someone."

"I'm not doolally, Karen. I'm fine."

"So what's all this stuff about angels?"

I hesitated. "It was nothing to worry about—it was a sort of game."

"A game? Thomas, love, I'm a busy woman. I've got a career to think of."

"I know. I'm sorry. Could you send me back the key?"

Grumbling, she took down my address.

"Will we be able to talk now and then?" I asked.

"Yeah. I'm coming down to London soon. Maybe we could go and have a meal."

"That'd be good."

"I'd better go now, love. I'm on stage soon."

"Say hi to the Great Miraculo for me."

She laughed. "Bloomin' kids," she said.

33 · FALLEN

IT WAS A TIME FOR NORMALITY, for starting again. Ten days remained before the start of the autumn term. The Wisdom family spent most of that time doing something the Wisdom family had never been particularly good at—it slobbed out.

Mum and Dad sat in the garden, chatting and drinking wine. Amy went out with Luke a couple more times, then told us kind of tearfully that she had broken up with him because she had decided that (hey, surprise!) he was a tad boring. I watched TV and read and enjoyed not having to worry about the future of mankind for a change.

I was, of course, missing Gip. Although I was no longer on a guilt trip about what I had done, I kept remembering times we had in the past, jokes I could make which only Gip really understood. I rang another friend, a guy called Matt, even went round his place to check out a new computer game he had been given for his birthday.

It was fine. It was good. Matt was a perfectly OK guy, his new game was great and his stories about meeting up with some girl he met on a camping holiday in France were kind of funny, if a little tame compared to what I had been doing that summer.

I listened and smiled and knew that I would be doing a lot of listening and smiling over the next few weeks. For the past few years, I had belonged to an exclusive club—with a membership of two. Now that club was closed and it was time for me to mix and match and make new friends. Like Mum, Dad, and Amy, I had to get human.

During that time, I avoided the corner of the park where Gip and I used to go. It was a place with too many memories. Then, on the day before school began, I decided that the only way to move into a new future was to face up to the past.

It was early evening, all gold and sad with a hint of chill in the air. I had slipped out of the house with Dougal, not telling anyone where I was going. I entered the park, sauntered past a group of kids playing football. I went to the bench behind the hut, our bench.

I looked around me, breathing heavily, my mind full of thoughts and echoes and regrets. I watched my dog as he scuttled about the undergrowth among the first leaves of autumn. I must have sat there for ten, maybe fifteen minutes.

It was getting cold. I called Dougal. Reluctantly, he made his way back to me. Then, suddenly, he stopped some five yards short of the bench where I sat. He growled, the hackles on his back rising.

"Hey, Doogie," I said. "Cut it out, what's your problem?"

I noticed that he was not looking at me but at a point

behind me. I was about to look over my shoulder when I heard a voice that I knew better than any other.

"I'm his problem."

Slowly, I turned. A figure was standing behind me, still and threatening. In one hand, glinting in the evening sun, was a knife.

"Gip," I said.

He stared at me in silence.

"How's it going then?" I asked.

He walked forward slowly, his eyes fixed on mine. As he reached the bench, he raised the knife to no more than a few inches from my throat. He sat down beside me.

"How d'you think it's going?" he asked huskily.

"You're alive," I said, ignoring the blade as best I could. "I'm . . . I'm so glad."

"The guys in the squat got to me," he said.

"They were angels too?"

"Yeah. The house was wall-to-wall angel. They saw you going and broke the rules by bringing me back. Two minutes later and I would have been a goner."

"I did ring my father. I told them where you were."

"You're all heart."

"I'm . . . I'm sorry about killing you and all that."

"No problem. You did what you had to do."

I looked beyond Gip. The park was emptying as the evening gloom began to descend. In the old days, Gip and I would be glad that no one checked that the place was empty before the iron gates were locked. Now I longed for some park-keeper to pass by.

"What's with the blade?" I asked gently.

Gip turned the knife slowly, showing me, as if I had any doubt, that it was no toy. "Kitchen jobby," he said. "Does the business, no problem."

I looked him in the eye. "What business?" I said.

"You think you're in such great shape." It was a whisper of despair. "You won. Everyone's going to be nice and normal from now on. You'll be with your perfect family" —he sneered in the general direction of Dougal— "with your sappy little Scottie dog."

"We can still be friends. I've been missing you."

"It's over, dead. I'm leaving the area. There won't be no Gip at school tomorrow."

"Why?"

"I had a job to do. That's why I was here. I was to be Thomas's friend, his mate, his guide. They fixed me up, gave me a life, slipped me money. So I did it. We were friends, right?"

I nodded. "The best."

"But I failed. All I had to do was bring you into the Project and I blew it."

"Maybe that was because our friendship was stronger than any instruction the Presence could give you."

"Yeah yeah." He shook his head dismissively.

"You mean you only liked me because that was your job, because it was part of the Project?"

"No!" Gip jabbed the knife towards me and I felt the tip of the blade pricking my throat. "It had nothing to do with me being an angel."

"I know it didn't."

"When they brought me back, you know what they did?" Suddenly Gip slipped away from me and did an athletic little twirl. "They fixed my leg. Gip is gimpy no more. The deal was that I was to tell people that I had this miracle operation during the summer. And, hey guys, Gip Sanchez is a normal, regular guy." He sat down, jiggling the knife in his right hand, its blade a few inches from my ribs. "So if you make a break for it, I'd catch you, no sweat. I'm lightning these days."

"I'm going nowhere."

"Joke is, I don't want to be normal. I want to be the way I was. And, if I can't be, I'll just have to prove that angels can be human too. They can be good, like your mummy and daddy, and—" He prodded me with the blade. "They can be bad."

I looked at him. He was even thinner than he used to be. There were dark rings under his eyes and smears of dirt across his face as if he had been sleeping in the open.

"I'm a fallen angel," he said. "I'm ready to do the one thing that will make me free." He smiled down at the knife. "And then I will disappear. I'll start again somewhere new."

There was silence between us broken only by the rasping sound of Gip's breath. I looked into his eyes. I wanted to say something, to make him feel better but I sensed that I had lost him. He was beyond me, gone.

"You were the best friend anyone could ever have," I said. "Without you, I never would have made it. You saved me. You gave me the strength to do what I did."

Gip's eyes glittered in the semi-darkness.

Slowly, gently, I laid my hand on the blade of the knife, then edged it forward to the hilt. With a sigh, Gip released it. I placed it on the ground and, with my right foot, kicked it out of reach. Scared, Dougal jumped back with a yelp. In spite of myself, I laughed.

Gip shook his head in a way that reminded me of the times we had spent together in the past. "Your life, man," he said.

We sat in silence for a minute or two. Then he sniffed and wiped his nose with the back of his hand. "Gotta go," he said.

"Gip. Stay. Please. You're not an angel anymore. It's all past. Now we're just a couple of humans. We can be friends—normal friends."

He stood up. "Gotta go," he repeated. He turned and walked away, with such a lithe and easy gait that I had to smile.

"Think about it," I called after him.

He looked over his shoulder, smiled that old Gip smile, and kept walking.

34 · SPARK

SOMETIMES, LATE AT NIGHT, I go into the garden and gaze up at the stars. I think of the Presence, the Project. I wonder if somewhere, millions of miles away, they're looking down at us and shaking their heads (or whatever they have in the place of heads) as they watch poor old humankind blundering onwards in that hopeless way of ours. Do they feel sorry for the angels they left down here—Mum, Dad, Amy, Luke, Gip, Cy, Daisy Dover, the President of the United States? Or are they secretly jealous of the human world with all its faults, its precious sense of freedom?

At home, the angels became normal, all right. Dad and Mum set up a computer consulting business. Amy went slightly crazy and decided at kind of a late stage that she wanted to be a doctor. Dougal still believes that, deep down, he's a cat.

Now and then, from friends at school, I hear rumors that Gip is at a school on the other side of town. They say he's wild and kind of crazy and that he's a rebel hero for the younger kids, so I guess he never changed that much. I met Manny on the street the other day and he gave me Gip's new number. One day soon, I'm going to pluck up the courage to make that call.

Something strange—it was Amy who pointed it out to me. After their final visit to the factory, angels changed slightly in the way they looked and they behaved. A sort of light, a spark of humor and humanity, entered their eyes. Slowly, their marks of distinction, the derm upon their necks or shoulders or arms, began to fade.

But it seems they never quite disappear. There will always be a faint trace of what was there.

Take a look at those around you—your friends, your teachers, maybe even your parents. Check them out for that tell-tale shadow of what once made them different from you and me.

For they are all around us, the humans who once were angels.